My New Shirt

James M. Dyet

authorHOUSE®

AuthorHouse™ UK
1663 Liberty Drive
Bloomington, IN 47403 USA
www.authorhouse.co.uk
Phone: 0800.197.4150

Published by AuthorHouse 06/13/2015

ISBN: 978-1-5049-4335-2 (sc)
ISBN: 978-1-5049-4334-5 (hc)
ISBN: 978-1-5049-4336-9 (e)

Print information available on the last page.

This book is printed on acid-free paper.

My name is Joe Matthews, my story started when
a girl unexpectedly invited me to a party;
To make it a special occasion I
decided to buy a new shirt,
I never dreamed the shirt was possessed and how
powerful it would become. Right from the start the
shirt seemed possessive and as time went on I
feared for my safety and I was helpless against it.

Before I tell you the story of my new shirt, let me tell you about a village and a story told to me by an old gentleman called Harry White. This all happened about a year before I arrived in the village and he started his story like this.

Julie Spring was a sweet twenty four-year-old, long jet-black hair, slim and very trusting, she lived with her parents in a lovely cottage on the outskirts of the village and worked in the local shop, she was popular with all the locals who called her their pretty Angle. She spent some of her spare time popping into the homes of old people in the village and helped with their shopping, chores and had comforting chats with them.

Everything was wonderful until Henry Grass an eighty two-year-old local man who lived next to the local shop had a visit from an unsavoury character. The entire village thought the world of Henry and he was a favourite with young and old,

He would sit outside his front door and tell stories to children; the stories were all about his adventures with Rainbow an old fox that lives in his back garden.

Henry called him rainbow because he first appeared as a young cub, wet from the rain and at that moment a rainbow arched across the sky, he was probably an orphan, as he never left.

Henry also feeds two stray cats, Minnie and Sophie being the names of his mother and grandmother.

It all started one sunny afternoon when a stranger walked into the local shop and asked for the owner, who was Bill Carter and his wife Jill.

The stranger was a smartly dressed man in a suit aged about thirty-five and offered them £250.000 for the shop and adjoining property.

Bill told the man who introduced himself as Adrian Bush that it was not for sale and the adjoining property belonged to a man called Henry Grass.

Mr Bush left and shortly after Bill and Julie heard shouting outside the shop, Bill went to see what was going on and Julie his assistant stood in the doorway and watched.

Mr Bush was shouting at Henry because he would not sell and before Bill could step in, Mrs Ann Draper a stocky woman who lived next door to Henry started hitting the man with her handbag and shouted. "Leave him alone you bully."

The stranger grabbed her bag and this sprung Jack, Mrs Draper's dog, an old English Jack Russell into action, who promptly sunk his teeth into the stranger's ankle; Bill got Jack off and told the stranger to clear off and don't come back.

As the stranger limped away, he shouted that he would have Mrs Draper done for assault and her dog put down.

Mr Allan Harper, who looked a bit like a prizefighter and was the landlord of "The Drunks Retreat" across the road, had seen and witnessed everything; he came over, went to Mr Bush and told him that he and his customers would tell the police that he attacked the woman and the old man and then kicked the dog.

Mr Bush took a swing at Allan who knocked him to the ground with a left hook. The stranger got to his feet and without another word drove off at high speed.

Ann, Allan and Bill went to Henry to see if he was ok and find out what had happened, Henry patted Jack then said.

"He wanted to buy my cottage and when I said no the stranger got angry, I could never buy all the love and happiness

I have here with money, I want to stay here I'm so happy." Allan said as he put his hand on Henry's shoulder.

"Don't worry Henry he's gone now, I sent him off with a flea in his ear, well my fist."

"He offered me £250-000 for the shop and Henrys place, I Told him the shop wasn't for sale." Remarked Bill.

Three weeks passed and the village was back to its happy contented way of life. Julie was working in the shop talking to Ted White, a slim lad of twenty-five living with his parents at the flat over the blacksmiths where he worked.

Ted was in love with Julie and spent as much time with her as possible and did all he could to try and please her. They enjoyed walks and the odd movie at the cinema in the town; Ted was courting Julie and dearly wanted to marry her.

One day when Ted was sweet-talking Julie a stranger walked into the shop, straight away Julie called Bill. The Stranger was slim good looking and clean cut but he kept undressing Julie with his eyes, making her feel uncomfortable

"Can I help you?" Bill called out to the stranger.

"Just wondering if there is a guest house in the village? I want to rent a room for the next month."

"Clare Bell rents rooms out as she lives in a four bedroom house on her own."

"That sounds just the ticket, is she clean?"

"Her place is spotless, she's a lovely woman, I would marry her myself but don't tell the wife."

Bill told the man how to get there but not before he found out that the man was writing an article on old churches and their church was three hundred years old.

The next day the stranger walked into the shop.

"Hello my name is Paul, are all the women in the village as pretty as you are?"

He said to Julie, she blushed and said.

"I am Julie can I help you?"

"I need a loaf of bread and a tub of margarine, I would also like a jar of marmalade please, Julie."

"Help yourself everything is on the shelves and the margarine is in the chill cabinet Mr?"

"Paul Green, please call me Paul, perhaps we could go for a drink sometime?"

Julie quickly replied. "I am courting Ted, the man that was with me yesterday when you came in."

"It's only a drink Julie, sounds like this Ted has a ball and chain on you."

"I can do as I please, we aren't engaged yet."

"So you will come for a drink, how about tonight?"

"Just one drink then but that is all, only because I would like to hear about the article your writing."

"Where shall I meet you, perhaps I could pick you up from your house?"

"I will meet you outside the pub about 7pm; I don't like getting into strangers cars."

"Hope we won't be strangers for long, see you about 7pm."

Mr Green paid for his shopping and gave a big smile at Julie as he left.

Bill came out of the back of the shop looking concerned.

"Ted won't be very happy Julie, be very careful of Mr Green I don't trust him, he's much too sure of himself."

Ted came into the shop with a big smile on his face holding up two tickets.

"Look Julie, I finally got us tickets for the show you wanted to see in town, I told you I would."

"That's great Ted, what night?"

"Tonight at eight, we can catch the seven fifteen bus."

Julie went red in the face and looked annoyed.

"Does it have to be tonight, can't you change it?"

"Why not tonight? it's all you've talked about for weeks."

"Sorry Ted it was all a big shock, you caught me on the hop, I will see you at the bus stop at five past seven."

Julie was at the Pub at five to seven, she was wearing a mohair cardigan, silk blouse and jeans. Paul Green arrived at the same time wearing a suit and tie and stunk of after-shave.

"You look lovely Julie, how about a kiss? You would have looked better in a dress."

"Sorry Paul I can't have that drink with you, Ted has got a couple of tickets for the show in town tonight at 8pm."

"What the hell do you think you're playing at; tell your boyfriend you can't go."

"Sorry Paul perhaps tomorrow."

Julie rushed off to the bus stop where Ted was waiting.

"What was that bloke talking to you about Julie?"

"He asked if I wanted to go for a drink with him."

"Did you tell him you're spoken for?"

"I told him that the first day he arrived."

"I would prefer you kept away from him, he's after any woman he can get."

"Don't be stupid Ted you're just jealous."

Just then, Paul Green pulled up alongside in his car.

"Can I give you two a lift into town?"

"That's very kind of you Paul." Julie replied.

Ted grabbed Julie's arm and pulled her to him.

"No thanks we prefer to catch the bus."

Ted said in a firm voice and then gave Julie a cold look.

"Please your selves."

Green said with a big smile on his face.

"See you for that drink tomorrow as you agreed Julie."

Then he drove off grinning and looking pleased with himself.

"What are you playing at? He's a creep, he just wants to have it off with you, then go on to the next poor girl."

"Don't be so crude he knows we're courting."

"Then why is he sniffing round you and why don't you tell him to get lost?"

"You don't own me, I can have friends, even men friends and that's all Paul is."

"Enjoy the show" Ted said as he handed Julie the tickets.

"I think I will go and ask Fay if she wants to go for a drink, just as a friend of course."

"Don't you dare Ted, she's a tart, please let's go to the show I will tell Paul to keep away."

The bus arrived and not another word was spoken, both feeling confused, angry and wishing things were back as they were before Paul Green had shown up.

As they approached the theatre, seeing the bright lights and the happy look on other people's faces Ted gave Julie's hand a squeeze, he put his arm round her and gave her a kiss, Julie gave a smile and kissed him back. By the end of the show they felt very close and happy as they made their way back home.

The next day Julie arrived at the shop, ready for work and feeling very happy that all was ok with Ted.

As Julie reached the counter, Bill handed her an envelope with 'Julie Urgent' written on the front, she opened the envelope; it was from Paul Green and read. =Leaving the village in the next couple of days, please meet me at the pub at seven, it's not a date I just want to tell you something important, Paul=

Julie decided to go just to hear what was so urgent, she phoned Ted to ask him to accompany her. Ted's mother answered and said Ted had gone to the town on a job and she did not expect him back until late, Julie asked her to tell Ted to meet her at seven at the pub and tell him it is urgent and not to be late.

Julie arrived at the pub and sat at one of the benches out front hoping Ted would get there before Paul. Paul appeared round the corner with a big grin on his face and reaching her, he bent forward hoping for a kiss.

"Just tell me what's so urgent and stop trying to get fresh with me."

An angry look appeared on Paul's face, he then declared he needed a drink first and wanted Julie to go inside the pub with him.

"I am quite happy out here and Ted should be along shortly, hurry and get your drink."

Paul asked what she would like to drink, Julie asked for an orange juice but he ordered a Gin and orange hoping to get her tipsy. Allan the landlord put a glass of orange on the counter along with Paul's glass of bitter.

"Where's the Gin?" asked Paul.

"Try fixing her drinks again and I will knock you into next week,"

Said Allan clenching his fist.

Paul went red in the face, took the drinks and sat by Julie, when Julie asked what was so urgent he sounded annoyed and said.

"Don't talk shop and why didn't you wear a dress? I could have taken you to a club tonight"

"I haven't got a nice dress and I never go to clubs, Ted and I go for walks or sometimes to the pictures."

"Forget about Ted, I will take you into town and buy you a nice dress and then we can go out and enjoy ourselves."

Julie got up and went to the loo, when she returned Mr Green had downed his pint and asked Julie to drink up.

Julie picked up her glass, drank half then said she was going home, she had only gone about ten feet when she started to sway and stagger; she was disorientated as Paul steered her to his car, he got her in and drove off.

When Julie woke up it was late and getting dark, she was outside the gate of the church sitting on the grass verge, getting to her feet she picked up her handbag, then made her way home and went straight to bed with a blinding headache.

The next morning Julie was having breakfast when the front door bell rang, her mother showed a constable in who asked to see Julie; the police officer was from the town and not Mick Webb the local constable who is an Irish gent and could never pass the pub without calling in.

"Julie I would like to know where you were last evening and were you alone?" Asked the Constable.

"I was with Mr Green at the Drunk's Retreat then home, why are you asking, what's wrong?"

"Mr Green said you got annoyed because you never had a nice dress and could not afford one."

"It was Mr Green that got annoyed not me and since when has that been a crime."

"Never but stealing from the church is."

"What are you talking about I never went near the church."

"Mr Green said as he was driving you home you tried to get off with him and when he refused you got angry, you told him to pull over and then you got out at the church."

"That's a lie, it was the other way round he tried to get off with me, I can't remember leaving the pub and I came to outside the church, then made my way home."

"I understand you had a handbag with you, may I see it?"

Julie's mother picked up the bag from the hall and gave it to the constable.

The constable opened the bag, tipped the contents onto the table and spread it out.

Holding up a small cloth bag with a golden cross emblem on it, he said.

"I wonder how this got in your Handbag!"

He opened the cloth bag and found a small bundle of bank notes and a deposit slip the vicar had filled out.

Julie sat there speechless and her mother started crying and said.

"Why Julie? I would have given you the money."

"I never took that money it must have been Paul Green."

"You have the money not him, he seems to have plenty of his own and he seemed very worried about you, mainly because he never took you straight home."

"Why do you doubt me mum? You know I'm not like that."

"Your courting Ted, what was you doing out with this man?"

"He left a letter for me with Bill, It said he had something very urgent to tell me and meet him at the pub, I told Ted's mum to let Ted know."

"You went to the pub then a drove off with a stranger; I'm very disappointed in you."

"How well do you know this man Miss Julie, a good friend is he?" The constable asked in a stern voice.

"I know his name that is all really, he is just staying in the village for a month."

"You fancy the man then do you, that's why you went out with him and made advances to him in the car?"

"I never, why don't you believe me, please just give the money to the vicar and leave me alone."

"To much evidence against you and I have no choice but to charge you with theft, I will need a statement."

Julie started crying and all she could say was, she felt giddy when she was at the pub; the next thing she knew was, she was outside the church with a bad headache and made her way home.

"This does not look very good for you; I will have to put this case on hold for six weeks as I have to deal with another complicated case in the mean time."

The constable left and Julie got ready for work.

Julie was walking towards the shop and spotted Ted walking towards her but he crossed to the opposite side of the road without acknowledging her. Julie called to Ted but he just walked off.

Bill was standing in the shop doorway and handed Julie an envelope, then went into the shop closing the door behind him without saying a word.

Julie opened the envelope that contained her p60, wages and a note saying. (Sorry but because of what has happened she was not welcome in the shop anymore.)

Julie stood there crying as an ambulance with its siren going screeched to a halt out side Henry's cottage; to Julie's surprise Henry opened the door and the ambulance team rushed in past him.

"Henry what's up, are you ok?"

"It's my carer she just collapsed, why are you crying?"

"It*'s a* bit complicated.*"*

Just then, a paramedic called out to Henry.

"We need to know what happened just before she collapsed Mr Grass, could you come here please."

"Don't go away Julie and then we can talk."

Henry went inside and told the paramedics that Carol had arrived as usual; he was sitting in his armchair when Carol went to the kitchen to make then both a cup of tea. She had bought a cake as normal for us and called out from the kitchen, asking if she could try a bit, I said of course then a couple of minutes later she staggered in from the kitchen holding her throat and collapsed."

"The cake hasn't been touched Mr Grass."

Henry looked at the cake then looked around.

"Carol must have meant the sausages; the end has been cut off one of them."

One of the paramedic's examined the sausages and showed them to the other paramedic.

"Pretty sure they have been laced with poison, where did you get them?"

Just then, Julie came into the room.

"Allan who owns the pub sent them over for my supper."

"You don't eat meat, Allan knows that Henry." Julie remarked, sounding confused.

"Mr Green must have got it wrong."

"We have got to get this lady to hospital as quick as possible, it's lucky she never ate the whole sausage."

The paramedics soon had Carol in the ambulance and sped off.

Allan called out from the front door then appeared in the room looking surprised to see Henry there.

"Did you send sausages over to Henry for his supper?"

"Henry doesn't eat meat, I know rainbow does, but no I never sent them."

"Mr Green gave them to Henry and said you sent them, the paramedics think they are laced with poison."

"Julie, you know you had an orange juice in the pub and only drunk half, well old Joe finished it off and then collapsed shortly after."

"So did I when I got outside and couldn't remember a thing until I came to outside the church."

"Mr Green tried to get me to put vodka in your drink."

Shame you never kept the glass Allan" Remarked Henry.

"I did, I took it to the police, wait till I get my hands on him, he'll wish he had never been born."

Henry slumped into his chair groaned and put his hands over his face and started to cry.

"What's wrong Henry," Julie cried out.

"I nearly killed Rainbow, I was going to give him the sausages and I love him so much."

"I will bring a plate of sausages over for rainbow myself, would you like that Henry?"

Allan asked trying to comfort Henry. "You're all so kind, sorry Julie why were you crying?"

Julie told Henry and Allan what had happened and was very hurt that no one believed her.

"Doubt has to be put into peoples minds, it's not what you do it's what you appear to be doing." Allan remarked.

Henry reached out his hand and held Julie's hand.

"MR Green is a nasty piece of work, cunning and I think he might be a friend of that other nasty stranger, the one Allan decked and sent off with a flea in his ear."

Allan banged his fist on the table looking very angry.

"He tried to destroy the village shop and kill Henry just to get his hands on these properties."

Just then, a slim man appeared in the doorway.

"Hello your back constable." Said Allan.

"Your spot on MR Harper, Paul Green and Adrian Bush own a property business; we've been trying to get something on them for a long time." The police officer said with a big grin.

"Did you check the glass, had he laced the drink?"

"Yes, not poison but if Miss Julie had drunk the lot she would have been out cold for a couple of days and may even have gone into a coma."

"Have you arrested him?" Asked Julie.

"Yes before you good villagers got your hands on him and the hospital contacted me on the way here; Carol will be out of hospital in a couple of days, if she had eaten the whole sausage she'd be in the morgue now."

"Does that mean I'm in the clear?" remarked Julie.

"Of course, just stick to the people you know and trust."

Allan started to laugh. "Old Joe said he's sticking to alcohol from now on, orange juice is way to strong for him."

Mick Webb the constable appeared in the room and after asking if everyone was ok, he said.

"The charge against Paul Green would be attempted murder."

Julie stood outside the shop clutching her envelope when Bill appeared in the doorway, he walked up to Julie took the envelope and said.

"You're late Julie; Jill has just put the kettle on and got a nice fruit cake, she wants you to help her round the house today."

Julie gave Bill a hug, cried a bit more then heard Ted say.

"I can't turn my back for a minute and your at it again, can I have one?"

Julie turned and gave Ted a big hug and lots of kisses.

Ted smiled and said excitedly. "When you finish work we can pop to the town and I can buy you a dress for our trip to the coast."

Julie stood and looked at Ted in disbelief and nearly cried. "I love you very much Ted."

"Love you very much too, I'll see you later and my dad will take us in his car and stop at the jewellers before I buy you that dress."

"Not an engagement ring Ted?" Bill asked.

"Yes if Julie will accept it."

"Yes, oh yes please Ted, I will make you very happy and never give you cause to doubt me again."

Mick Webb put his hand on Julie's shoulder.

"Don't worry Julie just thought I would let you know the vicar refused to believe you took the money and tore us off a strip for even suggesting it."

Just then, Allan crossed the road with a plate of sausages for rainbow, as he gave them to Henry he took a bite out of one and said. "At least you know these are ok Henry."

The villagers all chipped in and they bought a rather long bench, this they put outside Henry's house for the children to sit on, for when Henry told his stories about the adventures he and Rainbow had had, which some times included Sophie and Minnie.

Ted and Julie got married in the local church the following year by the Dan the vicar, who by the way married Clare Bell, the vicar from the next village married Dan and Clare.

Carol the carer always brought a cake with her for her and Henry, just to be on the safe side.

The only one that never came up smelling of roses was Mike Webb; he had his normal pint then went to town, got drunk and spent the night locked up in the town jail for being drunk and disorderly.

Mrs Draper, Henry's neighbour started to spend most evenings at Henry's watching telly, or Henry would keep her amused with his stories. Allan arranged the odd coach outings for the locals.

In all it took two crooks to bring the village closer together and gave every one a better lease of life.

Henry has had a book published called.

"THE LIFE AND TIMES OF RAINBOW"

Now you know about the village; I will tell you
how I came to know those lovely people.

My name, Joe Matthews and I'm a slim 18yr old with black hair, I like music and am very easy going. I fell in love with Cheryl the first time I saw her, her shining chestnut hair flowing down over her shoulders first caught my eye, she was slim and pretty with eyes a rich hazel colour that matched her hair.

I was over the moon when she came up to me and told me she was seventeen years old and invited me to go to her birthday party, of course I jumped at the chance, she told me her address, smiled and told me to be there on Saturday at seven PM. I wanted to make a good impression so I decided to buy a nice new shirt that I had seen in a sale a couple of days ago.

I went to the shop the next day and saw a man was looking at the rail the shirt on offer was on; I the only one left was my size, I was disheartened when he took it.

The man smiled and went towards the counter but before he had taken more then three steps he let out a scream and dropped the shirt, he held his chest and collapsed. A woman rushed over to the man and shouted. "Get an ambulance, he's having a heart attack, I'm nurse." I watched as the nurse attended to the man and spotted another man pick up the shirt; he showed it to the women he was with and she nodded in agreement. As the man turned to go to the counter he bumped into a woman, he apologised and smiled and the woman smiled back in a flirty manner, this landed him a slap around the face from the woman he was with, who promptly headed for the exit looking angry?

The man threw the shirt back on the rail and caught up with her outside the shop and I could hear them arguing.

I grabbed the shirt, took it to the counter and then paid for the shirt feeling very pleased with myself.

As the assistant put the shirt in the carrier bag, the man on the floor got up and said. "I feel ok now"

He thanked the Nurse and as I was leaving, I heard him ask where the shirt was.

I rushed out the door and spotted the man and woman on their way back to the shop. The woman was saying sorry and she would buy him the shirt for being jealous.

I thought I had better get away from the store in case of any trouble, so I rushed along to the bus stop.

As I stood at the bus stop a man suddenly grabbed my bag containing my new shirt, he went to rush off but as he turned to run he head butted a lamp post knocking him self out. As he fell the bus pulled up, I grabbed my bag back and told the driver who looked concerned about the man lying on the pavement that he was a drunk. The driver said the drunk should be locked up and then drove off moaning about drunks and the like. As the bus rumbled along the street I thought about what had happened, I thought I was meant to have the shirt well, at leased that's what it looked like to me.

Saturday arrived, I felt excited about meeting Cheryl again. I went to the barbers for a trim and my mum ironed my best trousers and tie along with my new shirt.

I asked my mum what I should take to the party and what sort of present should I take her.

My mum remarked, as I don't know the girl I should get her a voucher to be on the safe side. My friend Mick was going into town so I got a lift there and back to get the voucher.

The day passed quickly and I arrived at Cheryl's feeling on top of the world, I knocked and waited, a middle-aged woman opened the door, smiled, invited me in and showed me into the lounge.

I was the first to arrive and stood in the middle of the room clutching the birthday card and voucher, I looked round the room, there were oil paintings of birds and seaside views and in one corner, a grand piano with an oil painting of Cheryl and her parent's. A big floral Indian rug covered most of the middle of the room and a highly polished table and chairs were by the window, the catering was on a different table at the back of the room.

After about five to ten minutes, Cheryl appeared in the doorway and looked very pretty, wearing a light green dress with shoes to match and golden necklace. I was surprised to see she wore makeup as she had a lovely complexion and thought she looked better without. I asked if I was early because I was the only one here. Cheryl replied that I was the only one she had invited because she had not made any friends as she had been staying with her grandparents for the past few years. I never asked why, I was just glad I was with her but I did ask why she asked me to her party. Cheryl told me she had seen me about and wanted to see me again, as she fancied me. I felt my face glow with embarrassment, Cheryl just gave a cheeky grin and squeezed my hand before leading me to table with the food on it. She told me to help myself and would I like a drink. I asked for a cup of black coffee with sugar and I put two cheese sandwiches on a plate. When Cheryl came back with the coffee, she had a strange look on her face. When I asked if she was ok she gave me a big hug and kissed my neck. She stood back and looked concerned.

"Sorry it's all on your collar, I am sorry."

"What's on my collar?"

"My lipstick."

I went over to the mirror on the wall and saw a smudge of lipstick about two inches long on my collar.

"It looks like I cut my self shaving but don't worry."

"Take the shirt off, I will try and get wash it off."

As she went to undo my shirt buttons she lost her balance, swung round and grabbed the table to break her fall, she grabbed hold of the tablecloth but instead of breaking her fall just pulled the tablecloth and food off the table and onto her lap.

I looked down at her on the floor leaning back on her hands with tomato sauce salad dressing and jelly down the front of her dress and the tablecloth, dishes and food were in her lap.

"If you take your dress off, I will give it a wash Cheryl."

I said grinning, then I leaned forward to help her up and started to laugh but Cheryl looked angry.

Astride the food I put my arms under her armpits and pulled her to her feet.

"Would you like to take my dress off now Joe?"

"That's enough of that talk young lady."

Her mother called out as she entered the room. I let go of Cheryl and took a step backwards feeling awkward about the situation.

"What on earth have you been up to Cheryl? Look at the mess it's all ruined."

"Joe did it mum he tried to tear my dress off of me."

Her mother stared at me for an explanation; I just stood there speechless.

"You little liar, get cleaned up and spend the rest of the day in bed, go on before I lose my temper, you will get someone or yourself into serious trouble one day."

"I was only joking mum, honest, Joe tell my mum what happened please, she never believes me."

I explained to her mother what happened and we just tried to make light of the situation, so it would not ruin her birthday.

I kept wondering what would have happened if her mother had believed her and I had been arrested.

Her mum told Cheryl to go and change while she cleared the mess up.

I asked her mother the reason she knew Cheryl had lied about me.

"Why do you think she spent the last few years with her grandparents?"

"I don't know."

"Cheryl makes things up, I sent her away after she stole money from my purse and said her father took it."

"Did she tell you she made it up?"

"No, it was lucky my husband's friend was waiting in the hall, he saw her take it."

"But why would she accuse her father."

"He refused to let her go out with a boy who was known for sleeping around and getting into trouble with the police."

"But why pick on me? I haven't done anything to her."

"She ruined her dress, that would be enough for her to turn on you, you're lucky it happened here young man."

"She would have told them the truth though wouldn't she?"

"No! Not once she has told a lie, unless she's been found out like just now, when I heard you two talking."

I could not believe some one so lovely could be so nasty. Everything was great until she tried to take my shirt off then everything fell apart.

"I think I had better leave, only I feel unsettled and it's like a lovely dream that's turned into a nightmare."

"I understand Joe, here take the voucher back, perhaps you had better go before she comes down."

I left the voucher and left feeling very lonely and sad about the whole affair.

All I wanted to do was get home, get something to eat and watch a film to take my mind off Cheryl.

I started walking down the road to take a short cut through the woods when a car tooted and pulled along side asking me for directions. The man was going about fifteen miles the other side of the village I lived in and could not grasp the directions, he had a Scottish accent, he was a chubby man and wore a chunky woollen cardigan and trilby hat. The man said if I went with him to show him the way he would give me a fiver and drop me home on his way back.

Seemed just what the doctor ordered so I agreed and we drove off at high speed.

The man hardly spoke and just concentrated on the directions. By the time, we arrived at his destination it had started to get dark; he dropped off a package and started back.

The man said his name was Allan and said he knew a short cut back. We seemed to be driving for a long time and I no longer recognised where I was, Allan said. "I think we're lost."

All I could see were trees and it seemed we were driving through a forest in the middle of nowhere; Allan put the courtesy light on and gave me a map hoping I could find where we were, while I was looking at the map Allan turned to look at me, he grabbed my shirt collar and said.

"Lipstick, you lucky chap."

As he grabbed hold of the collar there was a bang so he pulled over at the side of the road.

"Blast! Got a puncher, good job it's not raining."

Allan went to the boot and got out the spare wheel only to find it was flat, but he said he had a pump. He didn't want a hand but suggested I had a catnap on the back seat and he would wake me up when we reached my home, so I did. I felt the car drop back down, so while Allan was tightening the nuts

I got out and walked over to the trees for a call of nature. As I finished I heard a car engine, I looked over the road and saw Allan speed off thinking I was still asleep on the back seat.

Allan was in for a shock when he goes to wake me.

I was stranded in the middle of this forest miles from anywhere. I started walking in the direction we had been travelling. The clouds only let the moonlight through briefly making it all forbidding and eerie. I walked and walked feeling hungry as the night dew started to make me cold and damp. I felt a bit dizzy and seeing a tree at the edge of the road put my left hand against it for support, I closed my eyes to rest them when I felt a weight on my shirt cuff.

I stepped back from the tree as the moon broke through the clouds revealing a large rat hanging from my cuff. Standing there in shock with my arm out stretched to terrified to move I stared at the rat and froze.

Although it felt like ages, in reality it was nearer ten seconds when the rat's eyes opened.

The rat's eyes were dark and radiated a cold evil look, the rat shook it's self and I could feel its teeth start to damage the cuff. In that split second, the biggest fox I had ever seen came from nowhere, it pounced from my right side and brushing against my chest engulfed the rat in its mouth then disappeared as quickly as it came.

I stood motionless for a couple minutes still feeling the fox's massive body against my chest and its gleaming coat in the moonlight inches from my face; I started to doubt it was a fox but I saw its face clearly and wondered how it got that big. I felt that I wanted to thank the fox in some way and for some reason felt humbled by his presence.

I kept away from the verge and carried on walking, I saw a car coming towards me so I flagged it down.

The car pulled over and the window wound down to revile a red-faced man.

"Sorry to trouble you but would you give me a lift to somewhere I can catch a bus in the morning."

"What are you doing stuck right out here son?"

"It's a long story but I can tell you how I got here if you give me a lift."

"Ok jump in, I will take you to the my village."

As I got in it smelt like a brewery and noticed he was wearing a police officer's uniform.

"Have you been to a fancy dress ball sir?"

"Don't call me sir my name is Mick Webb and no I am a real copper, if that's what you mean."

"Sorry, Just the unmarked car and err! You seem!"

"The word you're searching for is drunk, why do you think I'm on my way home this late at night."

I dropped the subject before I made things worse and upset him, I asked.

"Would you mind if I slept in one of your cells till I catch the bus in the morning."

"Certainly not, Clare Bell will put you up she has a guest house, lovely lady, she married Dan our vicar."

"I don't have much money, not even sure if I have enough to get home; in fact I haven't got a clue where I am."

"Leave it to me, what's your name son."

"Joe Matthews, you're really kind, you put my faith back in the great British bobby."

"Are you taking the Mickey out of me because I've been drinking?"

"No I think you're great, you have given me a lift and getting me a bed for the night, well at least I hope you are."

"Your ok kid, Sorry I mean Joe, soon be there."

Well his soon was about twenty-five minutes in the opposite direction winding down narrow lanes.

"It seems a long way Mick."

"By the road it is, not far as we have cut through the woods as the crow flies."

It was late and dark when we arrived at Mrs Bells, which was on the edge of some woods; the only light was from the coach lamp in the front porch. Mick walked surprisingly in a dead straight line to the front door and knocked rather loudly.

A light came on in one of the upstairs rooms and the window opened.

"I know that's you Mick, one day you'll knock the door down, what's up now?"

"Sorry to disturb you Clare, this young man needs your help, like a bed for the night."

"Hang on; I'll be down in a minute."

The window shut and a few minutes later the hall light came on, the door opened and there stood a woman with a face like an angle, flowing golden hair and eyes full of loving-kindness. Come in young man you must be intoxicated being with our Mick, you look like you could do with some hot soup."

"Before you help me Mrs Bell I must tell you I can't pay you straight away, I could send it to you once I get home but I will understand if you say no."

"Mrs Taylor, Bell was my maiden name, it's a wonder Mick can remember his own name."

I stood there hoping she would accept my proposal. Mrs Taylor looked straight into my eyes and smiled.

"Mr Taylor must be the luckiest man alive to have someone as lovely as you."

I suddenly realised what I had said and felt embarrassed.

"Rev Taylor young man and yes I still thank the lord for giving me my darling Clare."

I turned to see a very happy looking man standing in the hall doorway.

"I could smell you all the way up stairs Mick, I think we can all do with a drink and you can tell us how you came to be in this situation."

"Before we go any further my name is Clare and this lovely man is Dan unless he wants to be Rev Taylor."

"Just Dan when I haven't got my collar on."

We all sat at a big table in the kitchen and everyone had tea, I had some delicious home made soup which warmed me up.

I told them what had happened and when I finished they all smiled and Clare said.

"I want you to meet someone you already know and a great old man who will want to hear this."

"Who do I know? I've never been to this village before."

"All I will say is Rainbow now let me show you your bed, after you have phoned your mother."

"Is it alright to send you the money?"

"Just get to bed or you won't get any sleep before breakfast."

As soon as I snuggled under the blankets and my head sunk into the pillow I drifted into a lovely asleep.

Next thing I knew was there was a knock on the bedroom door, as it opened I heard the Rev Taylor call out.

"Up you get Romeo, breakfast is ready."

I got up and was surprised to find I was wearing my shirt, mainly because I had hung it on the chair before getting into bed. I went down to the hall and before going into the kitchen, I felt scruffy with lipstick on my collar. There was a large golden framed mirror in the hall, I looked in it only to find my collar was clean, I looked at my cuff and the rat's teeth marks were gone.

I went into the kitchen and to my surprise Mick was sitting at the table with a big mug of coffee.

"Hello Mick you're an early bird, thanks again for what you've done."

"He never left, good job he passed out here and not on the way here, Dan had to pick him off the floor and put him on the settee for the night."

"I smiled; Mick looked comical as he hugged his mug of coffee.

Clare put a plate of eggs beans and fried bread in front of me; I was so hungry I soon finished my breakfast. After breakfast, Mick made his way home, Clare and Dan said they wanted to drive me to the village a few hundred yards up the lane.

We arrived at the village and pulled up outside the village shop but they took me to the cottage on the left. The dark green door of the cottage had a big brass Fox's head as a doorknocker.

A big long bench was about three feet away from the front door and stretched across the front of the cottage. I thought it looked out of place and thought it would look better outside the pub opposite.

As Clare knocked the door as I spotted the name of the pub. "The Drunks Retreat" I thought Mick would be at home there.

I heard a voice call out.

"The door is open come in."

Dan said he was off to the church and wished me well. Clare opened the front and I followed her into the living room that led into the kitchen. Clare pointed to a high-backed chair that had its back to us and said.

"Say hello to Henry, I think he will want to meet you."

As I walked up to the chair, I said.

"Hello my name is Joe nice to meet you."

I went to the front of the chair and froze.

Sitting upright in the chair was the large fox that had saved me from the rat. The fox looked me straight in the eye and stood on all four's in the chair, then jumping off backed me up to the chair until I sat down.

Although being scared to move in case it attacked me, I could not help thinking, what a magnificent animal.

The fox came right up to the chair and put his front paws astride my legs, its face came within a couple of inches of my face and sniffed my nose, my arms felt paralysed as his eyes penetrated mine.

In a trembling voice, I said.

"Thank you."

Without warning, a big wet tongue slid straight up the front of my nose and off the top of my brow. The Fox got down and disappeared out the back door.

"I see you have met Rainbow, are you ok? You look pale."

Clare laughed, remarking Rainbow had given me a fright.

"He scared me to death and you are right I had met him before."

"I new it was Rainbow that saved you from that Rat, another story for you Henry."

I looked around and saw a man standing in the doorway to the kitchen with a big smile on his face.

"Hello Joe, perhaps people will believe my story's about my adventures with Rainbow now."

"Does Rainbow come here often? He seems very tame."

"My Rainbow has been living with me since he was just a cub and that was nine years ago."

"I have never seen a Fox as large as Rainbow and his coat is really beautiful."

"Henry has fed him very well since the day he arrived and the vet comes to the house to give him his boosters etc."

"How wonderful, to have such a magnificent pet."

"Rainbow is not my pet but my best friend and goes wherever he wants."

"What about farmers they shoot foxes."

"They all know Rainbow, he saved two lambs from a strangers dog that had them cornered, Mrs Larking saw the whole thing."

"Tell Joe about Tiny Henry."

"Little Timmy lost his pet guinea Pig and everybody looked for the best part of the day, then when we all sat down for a rest and have a cup of tea Rainbow walked in, put his paws on the table and carefully placed Tiny on the table in front of Timmy."

"Henry is pleased that Rainbow has never killed anything."

"What about the Rat Rainbow saved me from."

"My Rainbow would have dropped it off in the woods alive; he's just a big softy."

Henry made us a cup of tea and a piece of cake his carer had left for him.

After hearing a couple more of Rainbows adventures Clare asked if I would like to go with her to the shop, so we thanked Henry and left.

The shop was only next door, a quaint little village shop, which threw you back to yesteryear.

A very pretty, cheerful young woman called Julie served us; I did notice she was wearing a wedding ring. I thought what a lucky bloke her husband was.

Clare paid for her shopping then asked if I would stay for dinner and then she would drive me home.

Clare made a lovely dinner then we all relaxed to let our dinner settle. As Clare put our drinks on the coffee table an old gentleman came in and we got talking. He told me how two land developers tried to buy the shop and Henry's cottage. You know what he told me at the beginning of this story, his name, Harry White, everyone called him the local rag as he knew everyone's business, apparently he just does odd jobs and pops in to Clare's for a chat and a free cuppa.

After he told me the story, he left taking a bun with him.

Clare said. "Everything he told you about the poison sausages and the rest is true, but it all worked out well in the end."

We set off about an hour later armed with a flask of coffee and a road map; we had been driving about forty minutes when Clare pulled up at a petrol station.

I got out the car to stretch my legs and went into the garage shop to get some chewing gum. As I was looking at the different types of chewing gum on the shelf a man with tattooed arms and gold chains round his neck came in, he started laughing as he noticed my clean white shirt and remarked it needed soiling. The man seemed rather full of himself as he came over and pulled at my collar.

"Get your hands off my shirt, its bad luck."

"Oh yea, I don't believe in bad luck."

Just as he said that the woman serving called to the man.

"Is that your big BMW SIR?"

"What of it Lady."

"It is rolling away perhaps you should put the handbrake on next time sir."

The man ran out of the shop just in time to see an articulated lorry smash into the side of his BMW as it rolled into the duel carriageway, he stood motionless for a few seconds, turned and then came back into the shop, he stared at me then went red in the face as he clenched his fists.

"The handbrake was on you did this."

The man grabbed hold of the front of my shirt then pulled his fist back but I swung him round making him loose his balance hitting his head on the drinks cabinet, he fell knocking a bottle of milk over. Picking up the bottle half filled with milk, he threw the milk over my shirt.

"See what your shirt is going to do about that."

Just then, a big overweight man came bursting through the door looking very angry.

"Who owns that BMW?"

I pointed to the man still holding the empty bottle of milk, his smug look changed to shock. The big man rushed over to the man knocking the bottle out of his hand and landing his fist into his face.

"My truck is only two weeks old and the refrigerated compartment has stopped."

"It was his shirt that did it."

The man said as he struggled to his feet. The truck driver looked at me with milk still dripping off my shirt; I just shrugged my shoulders.

"He must think you're an idiot to believe something like that."

The lorry driver asked if I was ok as he grabbed the other man by the collar and dragged him outside.

"Did you see that crash Joe?"

Clare asked as she came in to pay for the fuel.

"Yes it is a shame; I think the man is a bit unbalanced."

"Why have you got milk over your shirt Joe?"

"That was the BMW owner that threw it over him madam but the police will be here soon, I called them."

Clare paid for her fuel and then we drove off before the police arrived. As we drove past the damaged vehicles, the BMW owner glanced at me bringing a big smile to my face.

Clare told me to take my shirt off as it was wet and put her coat on which was on the back seat. This I did then opened the window to shake the excess milk off my shirt. As the wind caught the shirt it flew out of my hands, I looked back to see it go high into the sky and disappear over the treetops.

"That's a shame Joe; I believe you were rather attached to it."

"I think it was attached to me, but I will miss it and what's more it cost £11 in the sale."

As we pulled up outside my home my mum rushed up to the car, I got out and she threw her arms round me then started crying saying she had been very worried.

We all went indoors and my mum gave me a shirt to put on before putting the kettle on.

When we sat down, I told my mum what had happened which surprised Clare, especially about the influence my shirt had had over the incidents.

About thirty-five minutes had passed when there was a knock on the front door; my mum opened the door revealing a well-dressed man asking if Joe Matthews lives here, I felt a feeling of dread thinking it was the police. My mum invited him in asking what he had called for; he saw me sitting beside Clare and smiled.

"Hello! Are you Joe? I am Cheryl's Father."

"Yes I am, is Cheryl ok?"

"Cheryl is in the car and she would like to know if you still want to go out with her, she is very upset."

I told Cheryl's father what had happened which made him look very angry.

"I apologise for my wife she is mentally disturbed, she seems to want to cause trouble for Cheryl, will it be ok to bring Cheryl in."

My mum nodded to him then he went out to get Cheryl. Clare got up and said she was going home; I offered Clare fifty pounds for all she had done for me but she refused. She gave me a big hug and told me to look her up again soon. As Clare went to her car she passed Cheryl, said something to her and waved to us all as she drove off.

Cheryl came up to me and gave me a hug then we all went indoors. I felt good that I was back with Cheryl. After sorting things out, I arranged to meet Cheryl the following evening.

After they left I realised I still had Clare's coat and that meant I would have to try to return it. That night I had a good sleep dreaming of what had gone on, wondering if it had all been a dream.

Next Morning I got up, had my breakfast and got ready for work. As I walked away from the house I looked back and could not believe my eyes, drifting down from the sky was the shirt, it floated gently down and landed on our doorstep.

After going back and taking the shirt indoors, I went to work feeling happy that the shirt had returned to me and remembered the fun it had given me.

When I arrived home that evening my mother handed me the shirt, she had washed and ironed it, I wanted to keep it for best so I took it upstairs and put it in the top drawer.

After dinner, my mum sat on the settee with me and we talked about my adventure. I kept remembering the village and the friends I had made there, Henry and rainbow left a mystical feeling in my memory and Mick the local constable makes me smile at the thought of him, even though he likes a drink, he's respected and has 100% backing from everyone in the village.

I felt exited at the thought of returning to the village and as Clare had forgotten her coat, I had the perfect excuse, so I decided to telephone her.

Clare said she would come, pick me up and take me to her guesthouse for the weekend. There are two reasons for this, one I never had a car and the second was although I was driven to the village and back, for some reason I never had a clue how to get there.

As I had the rest of the week to wait, I decided to give Cheryl a call and take her to the pictures. Cheryl was delighted and told me that her father would drive us to the cinema then bring us home after. It would have been nice to make our own way there and back but he meant well.

My mum wanted me to wear the new navy blue jumper she had bought me and had laid a light blue shirt next to the jumper thinking they would go together.

After having a shower and shave I slapped some after-shave on then picked up the shirt and put it on.

Before I could put the jumper on, my mum called out that the chip pan had caught fire. I raced down stairs and soaking a towel and threw it over the pan.

As I gave my mum a cuddle I said. "Best not leave the pan unattended in the future mum."

My mum pointed to the controls on the cooker, which were on the off position.

"At least you had the present of mind to turn it off mum."

"I wasn't using it, I never turned it on."

Feeling confused, I removed the wet tea towel and revealed some cold oil.

I looked at my mum, shrugged my shoulders and as I did so the oil made a popping sound sending a splatter of oil over my shirt.

"I think you had better wear your new shirt Joe, I think it's jealous and time is getting on, it's 5.30."

I felt the side of the chip pan and found it to be stone cold.

"You are spot on mum the pan is cold."

I took my blue shirt off and gave it to my mum to soak, then went upstairs to put my new shirt on.

I felt rather threatened, being my protector was one thing but being possessive was like making me a prisoner. What about Cheryl, would she be safe or not from the shirt?

I put the shirt on then my jumper and looking in the mirror noticed it had changed from white to light blue, I said.

"You were right you are a perfect match for the jumper, it will keep us both warm."

I felt a bit apprehensive as I said it not knowing how the shirt would react.

"It means a lot to me that you accept Cheryl and thank you for being my friend."

"Who are you talking to Joe" Called my mum from the bottom of the stairs.

"Just thinking out loud mum" I winked at the shirt in the mirror.

Mr. Ford arrived with Cheryl at 6pm, ran us to the cinema, and said he would return at 8pm to run us back home and then drove off. We got our tickets, some popcorn and sat in the back row.

The film was a thriller and as it was getting good four blokes sat in front of us swigging cans of lager they had smuggled in. When they noticed us trying to look round them to see the screen they stood up to be awkward.

"Give it a rest, can't see the film." I said hoping to calm the situation.

"What you going to do about it, here have a drink." He said as he threw some lager at me."

I smiled as I felt it running down my shirt, knowing he was about to cop something.

Cheryl wanted to leave but I told her to stay in her seat, then in a loud voice, I told them to sit down. The four lout's turned and started to climb over the seats to us, when the first slipped squashing his delicate parts on the arm of the seat and grabbing hold of one of his mates to break his fall made his mate hit his head on the way down. One of the two remaining lout's suddenly ran off to the toilet and the remaining one sat back down when I stood up and confronted him.

By this time, the manager was heading our way with two other men who quickly removed the lout's from the cinema. The rest of the evening went off well; we cuddled up together which felt like heaven.

Mr. Ford was waiting when we came out and took us to his home. Mrs. Ford apologized for the upset she had caused at Cheryl's birthday party. A buffet was waiting, In fact nearly the same as Cheryl's birthday party spread.

"What do you think? I hope it will make up for before." Mrs Ford asked.

I guess it was Mr Ford's idea and with any luck, things were well between them all.

Cheryl was the happiest I had seen her and so were her parents. Whatever Mr. Ford had done had worked.

It was time to go leave so I thanked Cheryl's parents for a wonderful evening.

"Hang on Joe, I will drive you home." Mr. Ford called out in a cheerful voice.

"Can I come as well dad? Please." Before her father could answer, Cheryl was already by the car.

On the way home, I asked Mr. Ford how he had managed it. He shrugged his shoulders and said.

"About 5.30pm my wife suddenly got all excited and came up with the idea."

"That's about the time I told my!"

"Told you're what?"

"Sorry just thinking out loud Mr Ford."

We arrived at my home and I gave Cheryl a kiss on the cheek, only, as her father was there, then I thanked Mr. Ford for the lift and went indoors.

My mum asked how I got on and was pleased all had gone well.

"Did your shirt behave itself tonight? Oh! Joe it's changed to light blue." My mum exclaimed with a big smile on her face.

"I think it influenced Mrs. Ford mum, because she suddenly thought of the party around half five, just about the time I told my shirt to be nice to Cheryl, as I really liked her."

"You are getting me worried Joe; do you really believe your shirt is possessed?"

"I know my shirt makes things happen, it protects me and makes me happy."

"Let me make you a drink to take to bed with you Joe, are you hungry?"

My mum sounded sad and seemed distant, I hope it's not about the shirt, I've been happy since I bought it. I took my malted hot chocolate drink up to bed, I felt confused about the way my mum had acted and found myself talking to my shirt.

"What's up with my mum she should be pleased I have you as a friend, she was wrong about you being jealous and possessive, how can I ease her mind?"

The shirt started to glow brightly as I took it off and hung it on the back of the chair. I turned to pull the bed covers back as a crashing sound came from downstairs; I rushed out of the door and headed downstairs.

My mum was lying on her back at the foot of the living room table; a broken flower vase was scattered roundabout her arm and blood was running down her arm from a large cut.

"Mum what happened? Don't move I will get a towel to put round your arm and telephone for an ambulance." I rushed out to the kitchen, as I was getting a clean towel from the drawer I heard my mum scream. Rushing back with the towel, I could see my mum still in the same place; my shirt was lying over her chest and injured arm and glowing brightly. She looked frightened as she stared at the shirt, then the glow vanished and she closed her eyes looking very peaceful. I lifted the shirt off her revealing no blood or cut and an unbroken vase. "Joe! Thank goodness you are here, have you phoned for an ambulance?"

"No need mum your fine let me help you up." I got her to her feet and sat her in a chair watching her stare at her arm. "I must have dreamt it but it all seemed so real Joe, I fell, the vase smashed cutting my arm, you went to get a towel and your Shirt appeared above me, it glowed as it dropped over me."

"No dream mum it all happened, even the vase is restored."

She put out her arm and ran her fingers down the shirt and smiled.

"I think I will go to bed Joe, I feel very tired, thank you both."

Watching my mum heading up the stairs I couldn't help wondering if all this had been staged by my shirt to win my mum over. I think this will be the last time I tell my shirt my concerns without thinking things out carefully. I finally got to bed but had a bad night worrying about my mum.

Next morning I went down stairs and was greeted from my now very cheerful mum.

"Morning Joe what a lovely sunny day, I slept like a log and feel better than I have for a long time."

"Glad your ok, did you hurt yourself when you fell last night."

"Come to think of it I never felt a thing, scared the life out of me when your shirt floated towards me."

I sat down without replying or said a word through breakfast; I had never seen my mum so alive.

I left for work and the rest of the week went by without any more incidents. Cheryl came round Wednesday night and Friday night and didn't seem to mind me going to Clare's for the weekend.

Clare phoned at 8.30am Saturday to tell me she would pick me up around 10am. My mum insisted I wore my best trousers and a cardigan and of course my new shirt. I thought I would wear my tweed jacket as it made me feel more relaxed.

Clare arrived at 10 minutes past ten and looked very pleased with her self. "Looks like you're already for the off Joe? Would your mother like to come for the weekend as well?"

"I will just pop back inside and ask."

I found my mum talking on the phone, she went red in the face and said to me.

"I thought you had gone? I will call you back later."

She told the person on the phone. "Anything wrong mum you look embarrassed?"

"I'm ok, what did you want? Are you still going with Clare?"

"Clare asked if you would like to come for the weekend as well."

"Perhaps next time, I have a few things to do today and a couple of things I need to sort out."

"Ok mum, I will see you Sunday night and I have left Clare's number by the phone."

After making mum's excuses we set off. I looked at Clare and felt honoured that these people had taken me into their lives making me feel happier than I had for a long time.

A little while into our journey, I must have dozed off because I opened my eyes and noticed unfamiliar surroundings.

"Back again sleepy head, I've just got to pick some things up from my friend George."

We arrived at a little village and as we drove through I noticed a man walking with a sheep by his side.

"Look Clare that sheep is walking alongside that man, just like a dog."

"That's Samuel and his best friend Penny; they live with George at his farm, that's where we're going."

Shortly after, we arrived at a farm, a big Staffordshire bull terrier walked over to the car.

"Is he ok Clare? He's a big lad."

"That's Bobby, George's dog a lovely gentle soul."

As we got out the car bobby wagged his tail and went to Clare for a fuss, then came over to me, stopped wagging his tail and stood with his front paws on my shoes. He looked up at me without making a move. I stayed motionless wondering what he was going to do, A deep voice called out.

"Don't worry; it's just his way of saying he likes you." I turned and there stood a very big man standing by the barn door.

"Make a fuss of him or he will stand on your feet till you do."

I did what the big man said and Bobby wagged his tail then wondered off into the house.

The big man came over, introduced himself as George and after giving Clare a quick hug asked if we would like a quick drink. We accepted his offer and sat in the kitchen, while

George was making the tea a woman walked in, she was short well rounded and very cheerful.

"Darling, Clare is here with Joe she told us about and Joe this is my lovely Alice."

"It's very nice to meet you, what a lovely place you have here."

As George put the tea on the big kitchen table, a slim pleasant woman walked in carrying an artist's easel. "I thought I smelt the tea pot, who have we here then?"

"You already know Clare and this is her friend Joe." George remarked.

"Hello Joe I am Tina, Samuels wife, very nice to meet you, is there enough in the pot for me George?"

"On its way Tina, have a seat and we can all catch up on our news."

I watched George as he put the mugs of tea on the table, his big hands dwarfing the mug's, he then went back to the worktop and came back with what I can only describe as a china plant pot with a handle on the side, his tea mug. As we sat at the table, a sheep walked in, came over to the table, picked a carrot off the table, walked over to George and put it on his lap.

"Hello sweetheart where is Samuel? And you know you don't have to ask."

He said as he gave her the carrot back and said. "Good Girl Penny."

Just then, a man entered through the back door.

"Just in time for a cuppa I see and penny has got her treat already."

"Samuel this is Clare's friend Joe, the one Rainbow rescued from the rat."

"I remember how do you do Joe? I see you have met everyone."

"Tea or coffee Samuel, or do you want some fruit juice?"

"Tea, thank you George."

"If you are wondering why George is making the tea Joe, it's because he insists on cooking everything himself and would you argue with him?"

"No; not even on the phone." George smiled and said.

"I may be big and strong Joe but even I wouldn't take on your shirt." And laughed.

I felt my face glow with embarrassment and took my mug of tea. Tina passed me the milk jug.

"No thanks I don't take milk but could you pass the sugar please?"

I kept quite and listened to them all talking and laughing. I thought how wonderful it was to be in the company of such nice people and the close friendship they had.

"Have you been painting Tina as you came in with your easel?"

Tina smiled went to her easel and handed me a painting of three pheasants, a male and two hens.

"What a wonderful painting. You are very talented."

"The male is called Bert; the hens are Rosy and Tulip. They all live on the farm as pets."

I stared at the painting full of admiration at the wonderful detail.

"I wish I could paint Tina, if I drew a horse it would look more like an elephant."

Tina laughed and said,

"Say it is an elephant that's what I do."

I laughed and thought what a wonderful person she is.

"Thank you for showing me your painting and the advice. I will give it a try."

I said as I handed the painting back to Tina.

"Would you like it Joe? Wait a minute I'll be right back."

Tina went to another room and came back with a painting of Penny and Bobby.

"I can't afford one of these, let alone both, not even if I saved up for ten years!"

"If you really like them you can have them to remember us by."

"I will treasure them; I have never owned a real painting, let alone something so beautiful."

Tina smiled took them from me and said.

"I will wrap them up for you Joe."

As I sat at the big kitchen table drinking my tea I felt a weight on my knee, I looked under the table and saw Penny resting her head on my knee.

"Hello Penny I am honoured."

Penny stood by my chair filling me with excitement; I had never been this close to a sheep before, she looked lovely, her eyes gave a knowing look as I stroked her head and I could swear she started to smile. Samuel came over to me, put his hand on my shoulder and said.

"Penny is a great judge of character Joe, so I hope you will come and see us all again, very soon."

"I would like that but how did you happen to have Penny as a pet."

"That's a long story Joe, it was Penny that changed all our lives and that includes Bobby's."

"My Alice has written a book about how Penny brought us all together"

George exclaimed excitedly.

"I will have to get that when it comes out, what's the book called George?"

"As the star of the book is Penny, Alice has simply called it Penny."

As Penny walked off Bobby came over and put his front paws on my shoes. I started to make a fuss of him when he broke wind, giving off a rather ghastly smell. Clare stood up and started to laugh.

"Come on Joe we had better make a move, all that remains is to load up the car."

"Sorry about that Joe, Bobby has a habit of doing that when he gets excited so let's get some fresh air."

We followed George outside after saying our goodbyes. George went to the barn, came out with a big bail of sheep's wool, and put it in Clare's car. Clare gave George an envelope and thanked him. As we went to get in the car Bert, Doris and Daisy came running down the yard.

"Here you are." George exclaimed, as he took a small bag of grain out of his pocket.

I took the bag and threw some behind the car, which Bert and his lady's, soon eat. The one George had pointed out, as Doris seemed a bit reluctant, where as daisy seemed very tame and taps on the back door with her beak for their breakfast.

Everyone came out and waved us goodbye as Penny sat beside Samuel and Bobby beside George.

"Thank you Clare I have really enjoyed meeting your friends, I was reluctant to shake George's hand in case my hand got crushed and my hand's look like a child's compared to his."

"George is a kind gentle man and loves animals, but he cannot tolerate bullies."

"Why has he got sheep in the back field if he loves animals?"

"He only has them for the wool, he would never have anything killed, in fact all the animals on his farm will die of old age."

I relaxed with a big smile on my face wishing I could win some money and have a safe sanctuary for some animals. We drove for what seemed ages but when we arrived at Clare's I realised I still could not remember the route we took or how to get to this village.

Dan, Clare's husband was sitting on the bench in the garden wearing his dog collar.

"Hello Joe nice to see you again, I will have to leave you both shortly as I have a christening this afternoon."

"We have picked up the wool from George; I will take Joe to meet Sylvia Clark and watch her use her loom."

"That's a great idea sweetheart; Sylvia will be pleased to see you and the wool." "Did you manage to knock a spot of lunch up for us Dan?"

"It's already laid out, just a salad with boiled free range eggs and crusty bread rolls."

"Thank you darling, come on Joe let's get stuck in."

After lunch, Carol drove us to 'The Thatched Cottage' where Sylvia Clark lived. The cottage was just outside the village in the clearing of some woods. Sylvia got her water from a well and the only light was from oil lamps as no gas, electricity or water services went to the property. Although she had no modern amenities, she was and looked very healthy.

"Hello Clare, who have you bought with you today?"

"This is Joe Matthews a very good friend of ours, come on Joe give me a hand with the wool, as it's a bit too heavy for me to lift on my own."

Clare opened the back of the car revealing the bail of wool. I saw George pick it up so I knew it was light and I said.

"Let me take it in for you Clare it's not heavy."

Clare stood there smiling, I grabbed hold of the tie ropes but got the impression that it was tied down.

"George made it look as light as a feather but I can't even budge it. As I spoke Sylvia came over to the car with a pair of wheels, once we all managed to heave the bail out of the car Sylvia wheeled it across the yard and into a small shed. As she disappeared into the shed, a gunshot echoed through the woods. Sylvia soon appeared looking very angry and headed in the direction of the gunshot. We followed and spotted a man with a shotgun chasing a small deer, I was horrified; I touched my shirt collar and said, "**Stop him**!" As I did, I saw my shirt glow. The man looked as if he started to fight off some flying insects; he put his shotgun against a tree to use both hands and as he did the shotgun went off discharging both barrels. The shot hit a big branch which came crashing down. The main bough smashed down on top of his shotgun breaking it in half and a smaller branch hit him across his head knocking him out. The deer stopped, looked in our direction then calmly walked off into the wood.

"Did your shirt do that Joe?" Clare asked. Sylvia looked at us both with amazement.

"What are you talking about Clare how could Joe's shirt do anything?"

"It's a long story but it seemed to glow as the man got attacked by invisible insects."

We all went over to the man who had just sat up holding his head. "Are you hurt?" Sylvia asked.

"I have a blinding headache but I'm ok, I can't understand how the gun went off!"

"You must have leaned it against the tree to hard; perhaps you should be a bit more careful next time?"

"Both barrels were empty; I had just fired both cartridges at the deer."

Sylvia stared at me and said.

"I think you have some explaining to do when we get back to my cottage."

We left the man holding his broken gun and looking near to tears and completely baffled.

No one spoke on the way back.

Sylvia put the kettle on a camping stove then looking concerned said.

"Well what is going on? I think I deserve an explanation, what's really going on?"

Before I could speak, Clare said.

"We haven't got a clue; Joe had told me about a film he had seen about a possessed shirt, so I thought it funny to pretend it was his." Sylvia smiled.

"A private joke between you two, I must have been off my head thinking you were serious, anyway Serves the man right, the coward."

Clare smiled at me and I smiled back with relief. The fewer people know about my shirt the better.

After tea, we watched Sylvia at her loom and then she showed us the different crafts she practised, Painting, jewellery and needlework.

By the time, we arrived back at Clare's it was 3.30pm. We had some cheese and onion sandwiches, followed by a black forest Gateau, which all went down a treat. Dan walked in just as we were finishing and looked disappointed he had missed out. Clare smiled, went to the kitchen and returned with his lunch bringing a smile back to his face.

"What have you two been up to today?" He asked as he sat at the table.

"We have been to see Sylvia; we've not long been back."

"Did you enjoy it Joe?"

"Yes thank you vicar, I found it very entertaining and informative."

"Very." remarked Clare, grinning.

"Call him Dan when he's at home."

After watching a film on television, we all retired to our beds.

Next morning was Sunday and Dan invited me to go to Sunday service. As the vicar and his wife were putting me up how could I refuse? As we sat down in the church, Clare remarked in a confident voice. "At least your shirt can't get up to mischief in here Joe."

The service went well until half way through, as the vicar was reading a parable from the bible about a lame man who had been healed by the laying on of hands, a man in the congregation shouted.

"What a load of old tripe, we aren't stupid?"

As he stood up, he lost his balance and fell on his left arm.

"My arm is broken and it's your fault talking a load of old rubbish, call an ambulance."

"I am the local constable sir and any more of this blaspheming and I will lock you up." said Mick Webb. Carroll Barr the local carer had a look at the man's arm. "That's a bad break on your left arm sir, perhaps you should think twice before attacking God in his own house."

The man said he was sorry and apologised to the vicar. The man held out his right hand to shake the vicar's hand as a way of saying no hard feelings.

The vicar agreed and as their hands locked, the man let out a cry and passed out.

The man soon recovered and announced, "My arm is ok." He went white as a sheet and ran out of the church. The vicar just stood there in shock, thinking a miracle had accrued, in reality I think the shirt had something to do with it, as it did with my mum. I have an open mind on all maters, it would be nice to think it was a miracle and as my shirt hadn't let off a glow when the incident happened, who knows. The man became a regular visitor to the church and the vicar somewhat a celebrity with the locals. In fact, the church had never been so full before.

After leaving the church, Clare and I went to pay Henry Grass and Rainbow a visit. Henry was sitting outside his cottage at a big bench the village had clubbed together and bought him, it was so he could tell the local children the adventures of Rainbow his fox. Five children were sitting at the bench all eager to hear the stories. Clare and I sat next to Henry who had just finished an adventure but was going to tell another.

"I will tell you about how Rainbow saved someone from a big rat called Horace.

My two cat's Minnie and Sophie decided they would venture into the woods and explore. It was late at night and the moon was bright, when not hidden by the clouds. As they went deeper into the woods, they spotted a stranger walking wearily along the road, which cut through the woods. They noticed Horace an extra large mean rat stalking the stranger. Horace was so big and vicious that even Minnie and Sophie Were too scared to tackle him themselves, so they returned home to tell Rainbow. Without a second thought, Rainbow set off in pursuit of Horace and save the stranger. Minnie and Sophie followed but could not keep up with Rainbow.

When Rainbow arrived at the spot Minnie and Sophie had last seen the stranger the moon was behind a cloud, he could see the stranger swaying about in the road but there was no sign of Horace anywhere. The woods were dark and as Rainbow lay in wait, he heard a sound behind him. He swung round, teeth bared ready to tackle Horace. The moon shone through the trees revealing Minnie and Sophie out of breath, eagerly watching Rainbow. "You two crouch down and be Quite." Rainbow told them and then carried on watching the stranger. The stranger staggered over to a tree, leaning against the trunk with his left hand. The moon went behind a cloud for a second then shone brightly, in that moment Horace leapt out of the dark underbrush sinking its teeth into the stranger's left shirt cuff. At that moment Rainbow sped towards the tree and pounced at Horace, his magnificent body skimming against the stranger's chest. Rainbow had grabbed Horace in his jaws and disappeared into the woods followed by Minnie and Sophie before the stranger new what had happened. Horace kept very still as Rainbow raced through the woods, knowing his teeth could crush him at any time. When Rainbow was far enough away he stopped and dropped Horace putting a paw on him to hold him down. "I will let you go this time Horace but never let me catch you trying to kill again." As he lifted his paw, Horace sped off without a word and disappeared. "Well done Rainbow that taught him a lesson." "Thank you both for fetching me." "That's how Rainbow saved a stranger from Horace." Henry remarked.

I stood up stroked Rainbow's head and turned to the children. "It's all true, because I was that stranger and Rainbow was the brave one who saved me."

The children started clapping and Rainbow quickly disappeared indoors.

"My Rainbow gets a bit embarrassed bless him and I think it's time for my dinner." Henry said goodbye to us and the children then went in to have his dinner. Clare suggested we went to the -Drunk's Retreat- for a drink and sandwich. Allan Harper the landlord was pleased to see Clare asking if the incident in the church was true.

"You wouldn't need to ask if you were in church now would you Allan." "Ok point taken, but is it true that the man's arm was mended?"

"Yes, come to your own conclusions to how, now change the subject."

"Ok I suppose you want your glass of wine Clare and what about you Joe, what would you like to drink? And how about some sandwiches Clare?"

Allan asked as he started to pour Clare's glass of wine.

"A glass of orange juice would be nice and I will pay for all this. Perhaps I could have a cheese salad sandwich and what would you like Clare?"

Clare said she would have the same. As we sat down with our drinks, Joe Brown came over to me and said.

"Last time I had orange juice it knocked me out cold."

"That'll teach you to take other peoples drinks you old drunk." Allan said jokingly. Joe looked up and smiled.

"You can laugh but don't forget you named your pub after me, you haven't got one named after you."

"Give me your glass and let me top it up for you, seeing you're so famous."

Allan said and topped up his beer glass then Allan headed for the kitchen to make our sandwiches.

After our snack, we thanked Allan then left. Henry had returned from having his dinner, he was just getting ready to tell another story. Some children were already sitting at the bench so we decided to listen to Henry's next tale.

"Let me tell you about my friend Cobb the squirrel and how he saved Timmy the little mouse from Horace. I had just fed the birds as I do first thing every morning. Rainbow had gone off for his usual stroll in the woods. Horace waited until Rainbow had disappeared from site before coming into the garden. Timmy spotted Horace and hid on the old bench.

He called out for help, trembling from fright as he called out repeatedly.

As Horace got nearer, all Timmy could do was keep quite and hide behind a pot on the bench, as he would surly be caught if he made a dash for his home. Horace had heard Timmy's cries for help and headed for the bench. As Horace was between him and his home, Timmy made a dash for my bird feeder. Timmy reached the bird feeder, climbed the pole and tried to hide in one of the caged bird feeders. Buster the

Robin could see what was going on and Spotting Cobb at the bottom of the garden, he decided to get him to help.

By this time, Timmy was in the bird feeder and Horace was already up the bird feeder trying to reach him.

Cobb flew into action; tore up the garden without another thought leapt from the garden table nearby and landed on top of the bird feeders trying to shake Horace off.

Horace lost his balance and dropped to the ground. Hearing me opening the back door he ran off, leaving Cobb feeling very pleased with himself."

"Thank you Cobb you saved my life, you were marvellous a real hero."

Timmy Said as he headed for his home.

I thought what a lovely story and how lucky the children were to have Henry. One of the children asked Henry if he gave Cobb a treat for saving Timmy from Horace. Henry smiled and replied. "Yes I gave him a big walnut which he really enjoyed." Timmy had appeared on the bench again and thanked Cob."

Clare tapped me on the shoulder.

"Come on Joe its time for us to go, let's get back as Jim is popping round with his little dog called Penny."

"That's two Penny's I know; what type of dog is she Clare?"

"You will find out when you meet them Joe, let's pop in the shop as I have to get some cat's milk for Penny." "Cat's milk I thought Penny was a dog!"

"She is but looks forward to some cat's milk when she comes to visit." On entering the shop, a voice asked. "What's your game? What do you want?" I looked at Clare and shrugged my shoulders, as the shop was empty. Clare smiled and laughed.

"It's only Willie pulling your leg look."

Clare pointed behind us at the window revealing Willie, an African Grey Parrot looking very cheeky.

"I see you have met our new edition to our family since you were here last Joe"

Bill remarked as he appeared from the back room.

"Yes Willie made me jump; I wonder if he knows what he's saying?"

"Watch it, don't be cheeky." Said Willie.

I went red in the face. A parrot had just told me off. Bill and Clare burst out laughing. "Willie can give back as good as you can give, Willie was my brothers and he owned a public house so don't get him started, especially as there is a lady present." "Sorry Willie, nice to meet you."

I said, but all Willie did was blow a big raspberry and give a chuckle.

"What can I get for you today Clare? I have some of those lovely cakes in you were after"

Exclaimed Bill as he placed a box of cherry bake-wells on the counter in front of Clare. "You know I can't resist them Bill, do you like them Joe?"

"Yes they are one of my favourites, I will buy them for you, it's the least I can do."

"That's kind of you Joe. I would like a couple of bottles of your cat's milk Bill and my loaf."

As we reached the door, Willie said.

"See you later"

I replied "Ok Willie"

A loud Raspberry came back in reply, followed by a chuckle.
"I think he likes you Joe"
Bill called out. I smiled back.
When we arrived at Clare's, Jim and his little dog Penny was waiting in the garden.

Penny is a lovely miniature Pincher who loves to run and she is so nosey. Penny's eyes nearly popped out when she spotted Clare pour her some cat's milk into a little bowl, which Clare keeps for Penny's visits. As Penny drank her milk, Clare put the kettle on and put the cakes on the table.

"Did you bring your photos of your other pets Jim?"

"Yes and its good to meet you Joe, I have heard a lot of good things about you; is that the famous shirt I have heard about; don't worry I won't touch it, I've been warned."

"Nice to meet you to Jim and little Penny; so you have brought along some pictures of your other pets; I would love to see them especially if they are as lovely as Penny."

That's Tigger & Scruff.

That's Tigger & Patch

Tigger is Very attached to patch, and loves Doris & Daisy.

That is Doris on his head and that is Daisy with her tail wrapped round Doris's tail, hanging down by Tigger's ear.

This is DIXIE and LUCY

I hope you can come and visit us all next time you stay at Clare's, Joe."

"I would love to and thank you for showing me the photos and bringing Penny."

Jim and Penny left leaving me with a smile on my face.

"You certainly have given me a day to remember Clare, I wish knew how I could show my appreciation."

"Sharing my friends with some one who enjoys their company as much as I do is reward enough Joe; how much longer I can keep this property is another thing, so next time you come I may have moved."

I suddenly felt very sad and emotional; I couldn't speak for a minute and Clare spotted the look on my face.

"Don't worry Joe we will still be around, somewhere in the village."

"Why have you got to move Clare? You love this place and the village would not be the same without you and your guest house."

"This is a very old and listed building; the repairs are costly and my savings are disappearing rather quicker than I had hoped; the tourist trade has dropped off so I have not much income."

"I feel quite hopeless Clare, I wish I could help."

"Your shirt seems to be glowing Joe, or am I imaging it."

"Your right it is, I wonder what's wrong."

As we looked at each other and shrugged our shoulders, the telephone rang. Clare answered it; she turned and looked confused, she said yes and hung up.

"What's happened Clare? I hope it's not bad news."

"A television crew want to come here and interview me; they had just received a tip about the tree at the bottom of my garden."

"Did they say what was so special about the tree that would cause all that interest, surly you would have known?"

"I have never seen anything at the bottom of the garden, there is no tree down there."

"Perhaps we had better check then phone them back and tell them they have got the wrong address."

"They called me by my name, let's go and I will show you there is no tree."

As we walked out the back door, we spotted a tree at the bottom of the garden stopping Clare in her tracks.

"What's going on Joe? That tree was not there this morning; oh! Joe, look at the trunk, I must be seeing things."

The tree was about ten feet high with a trunk in the shape of a face; the small twig sized branches looking like hair.

"I think your guest house will soon be overbooked with tourists, you won't have to move after all Clare."

Clare put her hand on my shirt and smiled.

"Thank you shirt I really can't thank you enough, thank you."

As she spoke a feeling of terror shot through me, realising the power of the shirt has grown too.

"Are you ok Joe? You look as white as a sheet."

I just nodded and stared at the tree, the bark protruded in the right places to give it eyes a nose and mouth, perhaps not in sharp detail but was unmistakeable.

As we were gazing at the tree Dan, Clare's husband called her from the back door and seeing the tree he walked down for a closer look."

"Where did that come from, is it real?"

He asked in disbelief.

"Yes sweetheart and a film crew are on their way, our money worries are over."

I wondered how this would affect the village in the respect of Henry, Rainbow and even Mick Webb the local copper who likes a drink. I had an awful feeling that it could kill off the characters in the village, who gave me special memories of the village life. The shirt might be responsible for destroying village life. I suppose that is why I am a bit of a loner and keep the special things in my life private.

"What's wrong with Joe Clare, he looks worried about something?"

I walked off back to the house, feeling every thing I loved about the village and the friends I had made here in the village would disappear.

"What have you done? The tree will kill the village, I know you meant well."

I said to the shirt, as I did the shirt glowed brightly and I felt my whole body tremble.

"Joe! Joe! Come quickly it's the tree it's turned to plastic, what's happened?"

"Thank you." I said quietly to my shirt and though I should give it a name. I walked down the garden to the tree and it had indeed turned to plastic. We heard the telephone ringing, Carol asked if I could run and answer it as her and Dan would not make it in time.

The film crew were phoning for directions, as they could not find the village on the map, when I asked the name of the village the line went dead, as I tried to get a dialling tone Clare came into the room and I explained what had happened.

"Don't worry Joe, perhaps it's for the best."

My shirt started to glow again and the telephone rang to my amazement, without thinking I answered it, a woman's voice said.

"I was trying to help, sorry Joe but tell her to look up the old blocked up chimney in the kitchen, I am Irene."

The phone went dead again so, I told Clare to show me the chimney.

The shirt had spoken to me through the phone and given me her name; it made me wonder who she was when alive. Luckily, the fireplace was only blocked off with a sheet of wood. All I had to do was take a few screws out. Dan fetched a torch, which I shone it up the chimney; I spotted a brick sticking out 2 inches from the rest. Reaching up I pulled it out and put my hand in the hole feeling a bag. It was a leather pouch containing a large ruby, four gold sovereigns and a gold pocket watch and chain. We all stared at the spoils on the kitchen table. Clare announced she would take them and get them valued, then asked me who the phone call was from.

"From someone that thinks the world of you."

"Who was it and how did they know about the chimney?"

I whispered to the shirt.

"Tingle if I Can Say." Which it did.

"The phone call was from Irene, who possesses my shirt."

"You gave your shirt a name, why a woman's name?"

"I was told her name by her on the phone just now." Clare nodded and said.

"Thank you both, I will go to town and get these valued with Dan."

"Good luck, I will block the fire place up while you're gone."

After blocking up the chimney, I went to the lounge and fell asleep in the armchair.

I was woken by the noise of the front door closing and Clare's voice calling me.

"Joe, you are right her name is Irene, and I have sold everything except the watch, look." I took the watch from Clare and opened it to reveal engraving. The inscription read. **TO DAD WITH LOVE IRENE X**

"It would appear the shirt or should I say Irene, intended you to come to our village from the first day you spotted the shirt."

"How old did they say the watch was? Perhaps we could identify her from the grave stones in the cemetery."

"I have a registry of all the burials in the cemetery; I will go and get it from the vestry." Dan said excitedly then left.

"The man in the jewellers said, that particular watch was made by Mr. James Canavan, he was a watchmaker from Scotland and always engraved his name and the date the watch was made on the inside of the back cover, in this case **10.6.1822**."

"I wonder how she died, people used to hide their valuables from thieves in odd places in those days, but why has she come back?"

"Good question Joe, we might get some answers once Dan brings the ledger."

"Why couldn't the film crew find the village on the map and you have never told me what the village is called?"

"Now and again outsiders stumble into the village because they have become lost. The reason we are not on the map is a mystery and the utility services send our bills but they all go to a p.o. box in the main town. William our local postman collects them and Utility Company's that need to come to the village have to meet William and follow him to the village. All they can remember about the journey is seeing the back of Williams's car, which is surrounded in fog.

As for the name of the village Joe, it's known locally as **(lost weald).**"

"I suppose it was called that because no one can find it."

"So the story goes Joe is, a witch turned up in the village in 1827, she fell in love with a man from the village, Tom Dickson.

Another woman was also in love with him and won his love from the witch Marian Setter, the witch cast a spell on the village, when the other woman had gone to visit her father in hospital down by the coast. Marian made the village invisible to anyone outside the village limits, the other woman never found her way back."

"That's sad; I suppose the witch married Tom Dickson?"

"No he found out what she had done and drugged her, he tied her to her horse and sent the horse galloping out of the village limits."

"Does that mean the witch couldn't find her way back as well?"

"Somehow she did, but Tom had already left in search for his love."

"At least there was a happy ending for Tom and his love."

"Marion Setter was really bitter; she cast a spell using clothing belonging to the other woman; a spell making her spirit earthbound until she fell in love with another. No one knows what happened to Tom Dickson."

"Does that work, or has it got to be another earth bound spirit?"

"No one knows but lately since you turned up here, every one in the village has remarked of feeling care free and brighter in them selves."

"Where did the witch live? Perhaps the answers to all this lies there, plus you haven't told me what happened to the witch."

"She lived in a small cottage on the edge of the field behind the church. The cottage is still there but no one has been near it since four men in 1828 went to the cottage to drive her out of the village."

"You mean it has a curse, something like that?"

"The men returned later suffering from amnesia and their hair had turned completely white. No one ever saw the witch from that day. People have been too scared to find out if she was still living there."

"Why don't we go and have a look, Irene seems more than a match for her."

"I will get my big torch as there has never been electricity at the property."

We were both tingling with excitement and fear of the unknown a we took a shortcut through the cemetery, Dan the Vicar, Clare's husband appeared in the doorway of the church and tried to talk us out of going to the cottage. Clare just told him not to worry, grabbed my hand and beckoned me on through the cemetery.

The old rusty gate creaked as we left the cemetery and entered the wood separating the church grounds from the cottage. The woodland looked ancient but a path had been trodden through the wood. Someone had been through the wood, yet according to Clare, the people in the village were terrified to enter the wood. I could finally see the field appearing through the trees and I could just make out a building.

The cottage was covered in ivy and a well was to the right of the cottage and looked as if it was still being used. Leaning against the wall was an old wheelbarrow, which seemed to have been used recently. We stood about four feet from the front door wondering if we should venture in or retreat. The front door although old was not covered in cobwebs, as one would expect, so I gave a loud knock on the door making us backspace a few feet. There was no answer so I tried the doorknob, I swung the door open as we stood there in panic, mainly because instead of a dusty decaying room, there was no dust or cobwebs and the place was spotless. There was no sign of any witches utensils or anything relating to a witch.

Clare pointed at the narrow stairs, I called from the bottom to see if anyone was up there, no one replied so we ventured up.

Apart from an old wardrobe and a bed, it was bare. The bed looked as if it was still being slept in and the patchwork quilt was dust free. On the other side of the stairs was a door but it was locked, we decided to go back down and have a look in the kitchen. As we started to descend the stairs, we heard the front door creak open then slam shut. We froze as panic set in, expecting a haggard old witch to appear at the bottom of the stairs. Seconds felt like minutes as we stared towards the bottom of the stairs until the front door opened and closed again, great we thought they have left. Tiptoeing down the stairs we both agreed to get back to the village as quickly as our legs could carry us. As we were half way across the living room, Clare grabbed my arm and pointed to the kitchen. The person did not leave but a second had entered the cottage, a tall dark haired man stood at the sink and a woman with brown shoulder length hair stood next to him, both appeared in their twenties and wearing old-fashioned clothes.

Unable to move, all we could do was stand and stare at them, waiting for them to spot us and wondering what the repercussions would be. The man looked sad but the woman although attractive appeared hard. The woman suddenly turned and glared at us with menacing eyes, without a word she muttered something, she shot her hands out towards at us.

My shirt glowed brighter than it had ever done before and a swirl of smoke that had flowed towards us from who I now assumed was Marion Setter the witch swirled round in front of us and back to the witch engulfing her. I expected her to disintegrate in front of our eyes but instead her face glowed, the hard look had gone from the woman's face, she was beautiful.

"My shirt feels different, you must be Irene."

The man looked in our direction smiled and took Irene in his arms kissing and hugging her.

"Thank you Joe, the witch was dying; she found us at the coast and took over my body. She drove my spirit out and brought Tom back here to live in this charmed cottage, locked in time and never grew old."

"Did you know the witch had taken over Irene Tom?"

"She made out she had lost her memory until she brought me here. If I left the cottage on my own I would age instantly."

"Someone has been visiting you here; we know that as the path trodden through the wood leads here from the church."

"She said that if I married her we could leave the cottage without growing old. I refused every time the vicar came here which was every month. I only love Irene and not just her body."

Clare shouted. "Wait a minute! Are you telling me the vicar was visiting here every month? Wait until I get hold of him. I will kick him out of my house and back to his church, how could he do this to me?"

"How do you know Mr Clothier? I was under the impression he was not from this area."

"I feel terrible, how could I have thought that of my Danny."

"Don't worry Clare I think we all jumped to that conclusion. From what I remember Peter Clothier is Dan's old school friend and his parish is in the next village, he married you."

"The witch had put a spell on him and if he did not keep coming every month he would be responsible for spreading disease in his village that would be wiped out. His only release from the spell would be if we were married."

"That's easily sorted, we will get him to marry you two and see what transpires."

Clare rushed off to fetch Dan. Irene and Tom looked very excited at the prospect of finally getting married. I on the other hand was getting concerned because my shirt was starting to tingle. As Irene's spirit had left the shirt, had it been replaced by Marion Setter the witch? I shouted to Irene.

"The shirt has started to tingle!"

"Quickly Joe, take it off before she completes the transfer."

I quickly took the shirt off, then threw it outside and closed the door.

"Don't worry Joe she has to be worn by someone to be able to use magic."

I waited outside to warn Carol and Dan not to go near the shirt on their return.

Dan married Tom and Irene and the instant Dan pronounced they were man and wife the cottage started to age and crumble.

"Everybody get out the ceiling is cracking, it's starting to collapse."

I shouted as a piece plaster hit the floor, narrowly missing me.

We all stood in the garden and watched as the cottage crumbled in front of our eyes. I looked at the happy couple and said.

"You are both unaffected, even though the spell that kept you young is gone."

"Joe is right Tom, we appear to be alive and solid and we're human again."

As she uttered those words, the roof collapsed with a mighty crash leaving just the shell standing of the cottage.

"That's your home gone, you will have to find somewhere to live, and try to explain who you are and that's not going to be easy."

"Don't worry Joe they can live with Dan and me, thanks to the money from Irene's jewels we can keep my house, I can do with some help round the place and so can Dan round the church."

"Thank you Clare you have all been so kind to us and we will be honoured to stay with and work for you."

"If the cottage hadn't fallen down I would have knocked it down myself, I had been cooped up with the witch for over 100yrs and I can't believe I am finally free and married to my lovely Irene."

We all made our way back to Clare's and had a meal. Irene was over the moon that she could actually eat and taste food again and Clare gave Irene her dad's watch back.

We all retired to our bedrooms, wondering if we would wake up and find out it had all been a weird and wonderful dream.

As soon as the sun streamed through my bedroom the next morning I was up, washed and was downstairs to see if it had all really happened. Clare was in the kitchen cooking breakfast.

"How many for breakfast today Clare? Three or five?"

"What ever do you mean Joe, why five, have you got some friends for breakfast?"

I guess the look of disappointment on my face made her laugh.

"I'm just pulling your leg Joe, Irene and Tom are having a lie in, after all Irene hasn't slept in a bed for over 100yrs, especially sharing it with a man."

Clare, Dan and I had finished our breakfast and were drinking our tea when the happy couple appeared; I have never seen such happiness as I did on their faces.

Irene insisted she washed the breakfast dishes up and Tom went off to fetch some logs for the agar stove.

"What time would you like me to drive you home Joe?"

"I promised my mum that I would be home for tea as I have work tomorrow, it's up to you when you kick me out."

"Stay for dinner and then you can spend a bit more time with Irene and Tom."

Irene was already familiar with the modern age, Tom on the other hand was not and when Dan switched the television on Tom nearly died of fright.

We could hardly refuse Dan's invitation to Sunday mass, which we all enjoyed as Dan always made his sermons light hearted and interesting, instead of the fire and brimstone sermons Irene and Tom had been used to in the past.

It was mid afternoon when it was time for me to leave. Irene thanked me and gave me a kiss on the cheek. She said she would miss me and told me to return soon.

Tom shook my hand, thanked me for my part in bringing them together and looked forward to sharing a flagon of ale with me.

We set off and although I longed to see my mother again, I was already missing my friends in the village.

When we pulled up outside my home Clare said she would carry the paintings in for me that Tina had so kindly given me. My mum was looking radiant, she was all dolled up and very happy. When we entered the living room, I found out why. My dad had decided to make one of his rare visits and although he lived apart from us, my mum was still very much in love with him. Although we both loved to see him, he leaves a deep sadness when he goes.

Clare stayed and had tea with us and we all admired the paintings. When it was time for Clare to leave, she handed me a book.

"A present from Alice Joe, read this and you will know how Penny the Lamb brought them altogether, Alice has signed the book for you, see you soon Joe."

After saying her goodbyes to my mum and me, she drove off.

My dad had a job to believe the stories I told him but once my mum told him what she had experienced with the shirt he was speechless. I never gave it a thought until he said. "Where is the shirt." The last time I saw the shirt was outside the witch's cottage on top of the wheelbarrow.

In a panic, I phoned Clare to get her to drop it down the well, reminding her not to let it touch her skin. Apparently, Dan had gone back to the cottage with the same thing in mind but it had disappeared. He searched the grounds but it was nowhere to be found and as the villagers were to scared to go near the cottage, the only one person sprang to mind was the vicar Peter Clothier from the other village. He would not have heard what had transpired at the cottage and had done his monthly visit. I went to bed to read the book Alice had given me named **PENNY**.

I sat in bed and picked up the book.

PENNY

**PENNEY THE LAMB
BEFRIENDED A MAN
AND SET OF A CHAIN OF EVENTS
THAT CHANGED HIS
LIFE FOREVER**

It all started on a spring morning, the sun was shining and the dew sparkled on the rich green grass and hedges as Samuel started to leave for work. Samuel astride his bicycle headed down the bumpy track from his cottage towards the lane. The fresh nip in the air gave a tingling feeling on his face and hands, a feeling of happiness warmed through his body. Great to be alive he thought and headed off down the hill towards the village as the church bells were striking seven.

Samuel prided himself he would be at the same place in the road dead on seven on his way to work, which was going past farmer George's field.

As he neared the five-bar gate at the bottom of farmer Georges field he spotted something sparkle at the side of the road and stopped to investigate.

Getting off his bicycle, he bent down to find a penny coin shining in the sun. He picked it up and noticed a very young lamb peering through the gate at him.

"Hello." Samuel said to the lamb.

To Samuel's surprise, he got a. "BAA." In reply.

He went over to the lamb that was on its own and noticed the rest of the sheep were at the top of the field. After making a quick fuss of the lamb, he said. "I think your name must be Penny" Holding his hand out, showed her the penny coin. Samuel smiled but as he looked into the lamb's eyes, he had a strange feeling come over him, a warm comfortable feeling of contentment. He got on his bike and as he headed off to work, he felt a bit confused about his feelings.

Samuel is married to a woman who treats him like a servant. His wife's name is Angie and soon puts a stop to anything that makes him happy. There was no love in their marriage or closeness and he had become a bit withdrawn.

Samuel worked in the village at the Manor as a gardener, so even his working life was mostly solitary.

He worked until four thirty PM every day except Sunday and always reached farmer George's field as the church bells struck five.

On the way home Samuel reached the five bar gate at the bottom of farmer George's field, he looked for Penny but there was no sign of her at the gate. Getting off his bicycle he leaned over the five bar gate and looked along the inside edge of the hedge but there was no sign of her.

As he turned to get on his bicycle he glanced towards the top of the field and spotted farmer George looking from his kitchen window.

The sheep were all at the top of the field, he Spotted Penny's white ears amongst the rest of the flock, as the rest of the flock all had black ears, he called out. "Penny"!

To Samuel's surprise, Penny ran down the field and put her head through the gate and Samuel went to make a fuss of her.

As Samuel put his hands on Penny's head, he felt a warm sensation go up his arm and spread across his chest. An unfamiliar feeling, something which Samuel could only translate as love, this was something he lacked in his life. This little lamb had made him realise how wonderful it was to be loved and wanted. It made him feel needed for the first time in years.

"Got to go now Penny, I will see you in the morning."

As Samuel got on his bike to go home, Penny gave a sad "BAA." Making Samuel wish he could take her home.

When Samuel arrived home, he had to get the dinner ready for Angie before she arrived home from work. Angie worked in London in an office, which was a very well paid job, yet despite this she sponged off Samuel's little pay packet leaving him nothing to spend on himself.

For the first time in years, Samuel felt good as he had something to look forward to, seeing Penny.

Angie arrived home and had her dinner, then told Samuel to wash up and iron her clothes for the morning. The rest of the evening, she would sit down in front of the television with a drink on her own.

Samuel finished his chores and did his sandwiches for the morning, he made him self a cup of tea and sat on the settee to watch the television with her. As soon as Samuel sat down Angie would look annoyed. She would turn the television off and pick up a book to read and ignore Samuel.

Angie often did that just to be nasty to Samuel and if Samuel asked her if, he could watch the television she would tell him to buy his own.

Samuel went to bed just to get away from the atmosphere, drained by this he soon fell asleep.

The next morning Samuel took his wife her cup of tea in bed and then he got ready for work. He put a couple of carrots in his lunch bag for Penny and then left.

The church bells were striking seven as he came down the lane; he could see the field from the top of the hill and saw Penny heading down towards the gate.

Penny loved the carrots; Samuel stood up pleased with himself when the farmer's voice bellowed out.

"Hey you, what are you doing there, what's going on? I want a word with you."

Samuel looked up and saw George striding down the track, annoyed and red in the face, George was a very grumpy man and his size made him look very intimidating.

"I have been watching you; what are you doing with that Lamb? That lamb is the runt of the flock; what did you feed it? Well I am waiting."

"We are friends." Said Samuel. "I just gave Penny a couple of carrots."

"Penny! You gave it a name, what's up with you it's a lamb not a pet, are you that lonely?"

Samuel just stood there looking sad then made a fuss of Penny; he looked at George and then looked at Penny, George slowly came over to the gate and bent down to touch the lamb; Penny Suddenly gave a screech as George got near and ran up the field towards the rest of the flock, looking back as she went.

George looked put out and confused, he looked at Samuel and without speaking another word headed back up the track to his house. Samuel wondered why the lamb was afraid of George and if George would stop him seeing Penny, Samuel watched Penny as she reached the rest of the flock; she turned round and just stood there looking down at him as he waved and left for work, he felt sad and wondered if he had lost Penny.

When Angie got home that evening and found no dinner ready she blew her top and called Samuel a lazy useless idiot.

Still feeling very upset about Penny Samuel just turned to go upstairs to bed and said nothing, this angered Angie even more; picking up an ornament of a beautiful Fairy belonging to Samuel she threw it at him; the ornament hit the doorframe and broke into pieces.

For the first time in his life he snapped, he threw the biggest piece of the ornament at the television,

The screen shattered causing Angie to scream and call him a mental case; he glared at Angie and went upstairs to bed.

Next morning when Samuel got up Angie had already left for work, she left a note telling Samuel he would be sorry and she would take legal advice about his actions.

Samuel screwed up the note then got ready and left for work.

When he arrived at farmer George's gate to his delight there stood penny, her little eyes sparkling;

Samuel climbed over the gate, took Penny in his arms, cuddled her and thanked her, he looked up and saw George looking from his window before moving out of site. After making a fuss of Penny and giving her a couple of carrots he started to leave for work, oh no! He thought as he noticed farmer George heading down the track towards him.

"Wait a moment, don't go" George cried out to Samuel as he raced down the track, Samuel stood at the bottom of the track thinking George was going to complain about him feeding Penny; instead, George reached Samuel and said.

"What did you give her?"

"Just a couple of carrots, she loves them."

"I gave her carrots, apples and everything I thought she would like, but she just backs away and only eats the grass."

"Penny must be afraid of you, why?"

"I don't know; I've never known a lamb to act like this one does to you, I wish I had a pet."

"Don't you have a dog or a cat"?

"Tried to buy a dog once but when I tried to pick it up it went for me."

"Sorry to hear that but I must get off to work."

Samuel looked round and spotted Penny running back up the field to the rest of the flock.

The day was a busy day for Samuel, spring always brings lots of work in the garden of the Manor, but on the way home, he noticed farmer George at the gate with a carrot in his hand trying to coax Penny.

"Still no luck with Penny then? Still keeping her distance I see, you could try one of the other lambs."

George turned round Red in the face and looking angry; without a word, he stormed back up the track.

Penny came to the gate and Samuel cuddled her; he gave her an apple then said, "See you in the morning"

To Samuel's surprise, Angie was home early and was getting her own dinner.

"I saw you at farmer George's; what are you up to playing around with the sheep?"

"Why are you home early Angie?"

"None of your business; make me some tea."

"Make it yourself, I'm fed up with you treating me like a servant, I go to work too."

"Think your big do you? Well you can sleep on the settee tonight and you can buy me a new television."

"With what? You take all my money, what do you do with yours? You never help with bills."

"I let you stay here in my cottage, how ungrateful you are."

"It's not your cottage, it belongs to the Manor where I work; it's a tied cottage so without my job we would be homeless."

"Just shut up and keep out of my way you idiot."

Samuel kept quiet and made himself something to eat, Angie finished her dinner then went out without saying a word. He sat down feeling very sad about his life and wondered what he was going to do about his marriage,

Angie never came home that night.

Samuel left the same time for work and made a fuss of Penny on the way helping him cope with his sadness. He enjoyed his work and Mr. and Mrs. Faye who owned the Manor thought a lot of him.

Mrs Faye always prided herself on her home cooking and supplied Samuel with plenty of tea and home made cakes while working.

Mr Faye often helped Samuel in the garden as they got on very well, this maybe because Mr Faye was also a bit of a loner and Samuel reminded MR Faye of his brother who had died young; he often called Samuel Dave by mistake.

This day Mrs Faye asked Samuel to be at the Manor at 1pm on the dot but never gave a reason.

Samuel made his way up to the kitchen door of the Manor and knocked at precisely 1pm, Mr Faye answered the door and said.

"Hello Samuel anything wrong?"

"Mrs Faye asked me to be here at 1pm on the dot."

"Strange; well you had better come in through to the dining room and see what my wife wants you for."

Samuel followed Mr Faye through the kitchen, into the hall then Mr Faye opened the dining room door and showed Samuel in, to his surprise, he saw a group of about eight people and four children looking at him.

"I am sorry to interrupt."

Samuel said going red in the face.

"Happy birthday Samuel."

They all cried out loudly.

Samuel just stood there in shock, Mrs Faye came up to Samuel, put her arms round him and said. "Happy birthday I made the cake myself, come over and meet some of my friends."

The women gave Samuel hugs and a peck on the cheek and the men shook his hand, the children just headed for the table, as they wanted to start on the nice spread.

Mr Faye came over and said.

"My wife found out your birthday from your p60, I hope you don't mind, we think of you as one of the family."

Samuel felt quite emotional and remarked that he was still single the last time he had a party.

Everyone had a good time and after the guests had left, Mr and Mrs Faye gave Samuel a present tied up in a silver box.

Samuel took the box with a big smile on his face and opened it.

"Thank you, it's a key! Thank you again for everything."

"Get the key and follow us Samuel."

Mrs Faye said excitingly as she headed towards the hall.

Still dazed from it all he followed her through the kitchen and into the yard, closely followed by Mr. Faye, finally ending up at the summerhouse.

Mr and Mrs Faye stood beside something covered over by a tarpaulin, Mr Faye pulled it off to reveal a brand new moped.

"It's all taxed and insured and full of fuel Samuel."

Mr Faye said excitedly as he put his arm round his wife's waist waiting to see Samuel's reaction.

Samuel stood there speechless, he held the handlebars then looked up with watery eyes.

"This day I will always remember, thank you both so very much, how could I ever repay you?"

"You already have Samuel, true friends are rare and loyalty even more rare, you have been both to us."

Mr Faye said pointing to the key.

"Come on Samuel give it a whirl, let's see you in action."

Samuel took the moped outside and started it up, he drove round and round the yard to the cheers of the happy couple.

On the way home Samuel showed Penny his moped, she much preferred his quite pushbike.

He arrived home and Angie suggested he sold it to buy her a new telly but Samuel said it belonged to his boss to save any arguments.

Weeks passed quickly as the summer run into autumn, Samuel spent longer with Penny reading books to her, she seemed to enjoy it as she snuggled up to him. Farmer George often watched from his house at the top of the field, looking a very lonely man.

It was the end of October; a cold and overcast day when Samuel set off to work, he was eager to give Penny her carrots and give her a lovely cuddle.

As Samuel neared the field, he noticed it was empty and reaching the gate called for Penny.

Feeling bewildered he flagged down Fred the postman and asked where the sheep could be. Fred suggested the slaughter wagon must have picked them up. Samuel got on his mopped and headed for the slaughterhouse two miles away.

Reaching the slaughterhouse Samuel rushed over to the office he was told by the receptionist that all the deliveries that morning had been processed. Samuel slowly walked back down the drive pushing his moped, torn with grief and his stomach painfully knotted he could not face work and headed back home. Passing the empty field he had grown to love, no longer would Penny's little face be peering through the gate and a rage burned inside him as he glared at farmer George's house.

Samuel just sat in the armchair day after day getting more depressed and withdrawn, barely eating and drinking enough to keep him self alive. Angie could not get him to talk to her and she suggested he would end up in a home before long.

Almost three weeks from that fateful day, Angie declared she was going to stay with her friend for a couple of weeks, as far as she is concerned he can rot away while she was gone.

The wind and rain was lashing against the cottage when Angie left at 6pm with her luggage. Samuel sat staring at the clock, almost an hour went by as the big hand flicked onto 6.50pm and a loud banging came from the front door.

"It's open, you never locked it." Samuel shouted out.

The door burst open to reveal a rather wet and very angry farmer George pointing a shotgun at Samuel.

"Haven't you done enough? Get out." Samuel shouted.

George grabbed Samuel's coat and threw it at him.

"You are coming with me, like it or not, get up."

Towering above Samuel and dripping with rain with a raging look in his eyes, Samuel had no choice but to do as George said.

George pushed Samuel outside and slammed the front door, then bundled Samuel into his Landrover.

The wind and rain lashed against the windows as George tore down the track and onto the lane.

George turned into his track and raced to the top but stopped beside the hay barn, he got out, opened the passenger's door and pointing the shotgun at Samuel told him to get out. George opened the barn door and pushed Samuel in, he put his shotgun against a stable and went over to light a lamp, as he did so he heard the gun hammer click on his shotgun. George turned to see Samuel holding the shotgun and looking slightly insane through grief and hunger Samuel swayed about and hardly had the strength to hold the gun up nearly falling over.

"You murderer, you killed my Penny, see how you like it."

As Samuel Spoke, he heard something that made him lower the shotgun; George took the shotgun and laid it on the ground, then guided Samuel into the stable, Samuel looked in disbelief; he saw Penny lying on the hay, she looked at him with sad eyes and as weak and ill as him.

Samuel dropped to his knees beside Penny hugging her as the tears streamed down his face.

"Why did you ignore my letters about Penny? I wrote to you telling you she was pining and would die if you refused to come and see her."

"Angie must have torn them up before I saw them, the postman told me the sheep had all been taken to the slaughterhouse and I don't understand what has happened?"

"I had forgotten the slaughter wagon was coming that day, there was a thumping on my door, when I opened it there stood Penny making an awful sound, she tugged at my trousers so I followed her and there were the slaughter men loading them on, I looked at Penny asking for my help, she seemed so helpless."

"What happened to the other sheep? Poor Penny they were her family, her mum was among them."

"I never let her down, I put them all in the back Pasture behind my house, I just wanted to make a living from the wool, nothing else."

"Penny still hates me for some reason, I never had a love like Penny has for you in my life and I really hope she will recover now."

She struggled to her feet and slowly went over to George, put her right hoof on George's left foot and gave a weak pitiful "BAA."

"Penny is thanking you George; thank you for saving her, you have her as a friend now."

"If Penny can take her hoof off my in growing toenail I would like to make a fuss of her."

After George had made a fuss of Penny, he left the barn but returned shortly with a feeding bottle and a cup of soup.

"See if you can get her to drink this? It should help get her strength back, the soup is for you."

"Would you mind if I stay with Penny tonight George?"

"You are staying with Penny tonight even if I have to nail the door shut, there are a couple of blankets in the corner, see you in the morning."

George gave a big contented smile and left.

Samuel and Penny had their supper, snuggled up together and both fell asleep.

Morning broke and the sun shone through the window and to Samuel's delight Penny was standing and eating the hay.

The door opened and the big shape of George appeared in the doorway, a big beaming smile on his face.

"Here you are Penny I've brought you some carrots for your breakfast and your breakfast is on the kitchen table Samuel."

Penny just stood there staring at the carrots.

"Its ok Penny, take the carrots." Samuel told her, with that Penny went over to George and started eating them, giving the odd glance back at Samuel for his approval.

"Good girl, I will bring you a bottle of special milk after we've eaten." George told her excitedly.

George beckoned to Samuel and he followed George to the house and into the kitchen, on the table was toast and two big steaming mugs of tea?

"Beans and eggs ok with you Samuel?"

"Thank you George, you've bean very kind to me and Penny, I don't know how to repay you."

"It's been so lonely the last few years on my own, when I rescued Penny something changed in me, all the bitterness seemed to disappear, I owe Penny a lot."

George said in a sad, distant voice.

"Do you mind if I see Penny every day George?"

"Anytime you want but you had better let your wife know you are ok, she must be wondering where you've got to, being out all night."

"Angie is away for a couple of weeks so I will be on my own."

"Why not let me drive you home to get some things and stay here for a while, would you like that?"

Samuel looked at George, he could hardly believe that this was the same fearsome aggressive man.

"I don't know what to say George, it's like a dream, you're a very thoughtful kind man and I feel so happy."

"Eat your breakfast and then after Penny has had her special milk I will run you home to collect some of your things."

After Penny had drunk her milk, she settled down in the barn and went to sleep, George shut the barn door and beckoned to Samuel to get into the Landrover.

As they neared the top of the drive to Samuel's cottage, they noticed a strange car, no one was in the car but the front door was open.

Samuel got out of the landrover and went through the front door to see who was there.

Angie was standing in the middle of the room looking red in the face and very angry.

"Where do you think you have you been all night? You haven't done the ironing, nothing, well what have you got to say?"

"Do it yourself, you're a lazy bully."

Just then, a man stepped out from behind the front door and pushing Samuel from behind said.

"I am going to give you a good hiding for talking to Angie like that."

He was a big man with greasy combed back hair and moustache, wearing a pin stripped suit and acting like a hard man, clenching his fist.

As the man got near Samuel, he grabbed hold of his shirt and pulled back his fist.

There was a big thud on the man's shoulder as George's hand crushed down causing the man to cry out in pain, George swung the man round and slapped him round the face sending the man sprawling across the floor and finally coming to a thud against the settee.

As the man rolled on his back, you could see George's hand print glowing on the man's cheek.

"Next time I will use my fist, I suggest you stay on the floor until Samuel Is ready to leave and he will not be coming back."

The man, Angie and Samuel were all staring at George in disbelief at his shear strength, the man looked terrified, probably for the first time in his life.

"Get a move on Samuel so we can get back to the farm, move it before I lose my temper."

Samuel turned and rushed upstairs, Angie sat down and started crying, the man just lay on the floor with George's handprint getting even redder on his face.

Samuel soon appeared with a couple of carrier bags full of clothes and a small transistor radio.

"We can come back tomorrow for the rest of your stuff Samuel."

"This is all I have George."

George was furious and glared at Angie.

"Come on Samuel let's get out of here."

"Don't leave me, please don't leave me." Angie cried out.

The man on the floor stared at Angie.

For a moment Samuel paused as he got to the open front door, George put his big hand in the middle of Sam's shoulder blades and pushed him outside, then slammed the door shut.

"Get in the motor Samuel, she had her chance and will never change that sort never do! How could she set her boyfriend on you, what a bitch."

They got back to the farm and had a big mug of hot chocolate, then Samuel said "Goodnight." and headed off to the barn to keep Penny Company and ponder over Angie's actions.

Next morning George woke Samuel up and gave him the bottle of special milk for Penny, George said. "Pop over afterwards for breakfast."

Samuel could smell George had been baking.

"I've just made some bread and rolls I have also made some vegetable soup, we can have that for mid morning with my home made bread."

"Do you do much cooking George?"

"I always have done, got a nice apple crumble cooking in the Agar."

"I would never have guessed you did your own cooking George, you don't look the sort."

"Josie lived with me, she was a bit like your wife and she left all the cooking and housework to me, what With working on the farm and doing all the chores it got too much for me."

"I never knew George, sounds like we both ended up with a bad one, have you had a divorce?"

"We never married we just lived together, I gave her it straight, start helping round the farm, or go."

"What happened, did she start to do her bit round the farm and help with the chores?"

"No she packed her stuff and left, she also stole £878 out of my safe, I never saw her again."

Just then, Penny walked into the kitchen and sat by Samuel resting her head against his leg.

"You're not allowed in the house Penny."

Samuel said thinking George would complain.

"Penny can go where ever she pleases Samuel."

Samuel smiled and thanked George but noticed George looked very sad.

"What's wrong George, are you ok?"

"It is great having you here, I just wish I had a pet of my own to love and make a fuss of."

After breakfast, George said he had to go out to see someone and would not be long.

When George arrived back, he asked Samuel into the kitchen. George made some tea then handed Samuel a letter, he opened the letter then Sam said.

"I feel so ashamed, I forgot all about Mr & Mrs Faye, I was so stricken with grief about Penny."

"They feel for you Samuel and totally understand, mind you they are hoping to see you back at work next week, they said the place seems lonely without you and the garden misses you to."

"Thank you George, how can I ever repay you?"

"You already you have, they have invited me round to tea and will be buying my eggs, I have made two new friends and customers in one go, how about that."

Things went well for the next two weeks, Samuel went back to work and George and Mrs Faye often spent time together swapping recipes.

George always looked sad when he saw how close Penny and Samuel were and still longed for a pet of his own.

George had a big open fireplace in the living room and one night he had made a roaring fire, both he and Samuel were dozing off in the heat of the fire feeling completely relaxed.

The tranquil silence was broken when Penny suddenly rushed in from the kitchen like something possessed, stamping her feet and Baaing loudly. George shot to his feet and rushed out to the kitchen grabbing his gun on the way.

Samuel felt rather confused and followed George out to the yard and then towards the back pasture.

A small cattle truck was by the five bar gate and a man was trying to get it open. George fired a shot in the air, the man's dog jumped in fright and leaped into the back of the trailer, the man quickly got in his cab not even taking the time to turn his lights on, he sped down the track to make his get away.

As the truck passed, George angrily smashed the butt of his gun through the driver's window.

"Do you know him George? He looked a bad sort."

Before George could answer, an almighty crash echoed through the night, which seamed to have come from the bottom of the lane.

Looking towards the lane, they saw two big headlights pointing towards the opposite side of the road, by the moonlight it looked like a big supermarket container lorry.

"Guess we had better see what has happened, perhaps Pearson crashed his wagon." said Samuel.

"I will just get my coat, you had better grab yours as well Samuel."

As they came back out of the house, they saw a man rushing up the track he cried out.

"Please help me, it wasn't my fault, he had no lights on and just appeared in front of me."

"Come in and phone the police and an ambulance."

"He's dead! What am I going to do? It wasn't my fault, he just appeared in my headlights."

"Calm down! He had just tried to steal my sheep and in his rush to get away he never put his lights on, don't worry we can vouch for you."

As they got to the front door, Samuel looked around and said.

"Where is Penny? He must have run her over."

George spotted Penny going down the track towards the lane and stopping just short of the bend.

George told the driver to go in the kitchen where he would find the telephone and then started to walk down the track towards Penny.

Penny disappeared round the bend, almost immediately reappearing with a limping dog walking beside her.

"It's Pearson's dog! It survived but it looks like its hurt."

The dog and Penny walked up to George, Penny backed away and the dog slumped onto George's left foot.

"My in growing toe nail, why that foot?"

George complained painfully.

The dog whined so George picked him up in his arms, as he did the dog-licked George's cheek.

"You got the dog you all ways wanted George, once a Staff bonds with someone it's for life."

We all went into the kitchen and found the driver was shaking and unable to use the telephone.

"Let me phone George while you see to your dog."

George nodded as tears of joy filled his eyes, after telephoning the police, Samuel made some tea then tried to console the driver.

George was examining the dog to see the extent of his injuries and luckily, it was just a sprain.

"You've got to give him a name now George."

George leaned down and whispered something in the dog's ear, the dog did no more than give George another lick on the cheek.

"Meet Bobby, my Bobby, my very own dog."

George shouted out loudly in great excitement.

The driver looked at George in amazement, he had just killed a man and the farmer is jumping for joy.

"Tell me about Pearson and how you know him George."

"I think you mean knew him, he was a nasty bit of work and enjoyed hurting animals, I broke his jaw once, He kicked his previous dog in front of me at one of the farmer's fairs."

"Did you get arrested for assault"?

"No! Mack the local copper said he saw the whole thing, he said he saw Pearson slip when he kicked his dog and hit his face on the side of the stall."

"What about the others at the fair? They must have seen you hit him and what happened."

"They all backed Mack's story and cheered when I decked him, every one hated him."

The police arrived at the farm and after taking statements they assured the driver he was in no way to blame for the accident. The police wanted to take Pearson's dog but George told them Pearson had stolen the dog from him last year, I nodded in agreement.

"You're my Bobby, your back home aren't you boy."

Bobby licked George again, one of the police officers patted George on the back and said.

"Lovely dog, glad you got him back, he looks like he was mistreated poor thing."

After making a fuss of Bobby, the police left with the driver.

"Thanks for backing me up about Bobby Samuel."

"It was Bobby that convinced them, not me."

George suddenly cried out in pain.

"He has stood on my left foot again, why do they pick on my ingrown toe nail, why that foot?"

"Drive me into town tomorrow and I will buy you a pair of metal toe cap boots and I will book you in at the chiropodist as I can afford it now."

George just smiled, shook Samuel's hand then went into the living room, he fell asleep in front of the fire with Bobby huddled up to him.

Next day Samuel did keep his promise, George never looked so happy and stood for ages in front of the store mirror admiring his boots.

Samuel managed to get George to leave and finally arrive at the chiropodist.

The chiropodist took one look at George and suggested he freeze the foot, as it would be painful cutting the nail, I think he feared George could lash out.

All went well and when they got home George sat down, Bobby went over and lay on George's left Boot.

"You did it Samuel all in one morning, problem is I don't think I can stand up long enough to cook the dinner my foot's coming to."

"Leave that to me, I will get you some pain killers, let's take your boots off before it really comes to."

Samuel helped George to the big sofa and gave George the painkillers. George lay down with Bobby and they soon fell asleep.

George, Bobby, Samuel and penny started going for long walks together over the fields.

They had never been so contented and happy and Bobby and Penny were best of friends.

One day when they went for a walk they came across two ladies sitting at the edge of the pasture, one was painting the landscape while the other was reading a book. George told them they were on his land and had not asked his permission, when they apologised he said it was ok as they were doing no harm, they thanked him and one of the women told us they were sisters. They made a fuss of Penny and Bobby and remarked how wonderful they were, this pleased George who promptly invited them up to the house for tea and some home made fruitcake, which they gladly accepted.

The sister who had been reading a book was Alice, a shorter plumper version of her sister and was an author, it was plain to see that she took an instant shine to George.

The other sister was Tina the artist and was slim, about the same height and same chestnut hair but she was more quiet and shy than Alice.

George asked Alice and Tina if they would like to come for Sunday dinner, they looked at each other, smiled and said they would love to.

Samuel asked where they lived and was shocked when they said -Hill Top Cottage-.

Samuel looked at George looking confused.

"Talk to you later Samuel, I have got a few things to tell you."

Alice and Tina had one more cup and some fruitcake then left.

"They are living in my cottage! What happened to Angie? I thought she was still living there."

"I told Mr and Mrs Faye what happened between you and Angie and you were staying here."

"You told them, why"?

"We all felt bitter about the way you were treated, Mr and Mrs Faye thinks the world of you, they couldn't stand the thought of Angie staying in their cottage after what happened."

"I guess it is for the best, I could never have gone back with her, she must have gone to live with that bloke and she'll come a cropper living with him."

George put his hand out to Samuel.

"Still friends are we Samuel."

"Always will be George, you are a really good friend, taking me in and looking after Penny and the rest of the flock, I always thought of you as a bad tempered aggressive man, how wrong I was."

"No you were right, I was until you and penny changed me."

Sunday soon came round and George started getting Sunday lunch ready, Samuel made them both a coffee and then went out to see Penny in the pasture, as George liked to be left alone when cooking.

As Samuel got to the pasture a smile came to his face, there was Bobby sitting with Penny in the middle of the flock of sheep, they looked like a couple of love birds; leaning against each other.

Samuel just stood by the gate watching and drinking his coffee, he kept thinking how great things were and what he had missed all those years with Angie, how he had stayed sane escaped him.

"Hello Samuel, sorry we are early, we thought we could help with the lunch, do the vegetables etc."

"Sorry Alice but George never allows anyone in the kitchen when he's cooking."

Tina got a small sketchpad out of her bag and smiled at Penny and Bobby.

"I have to do a sketch of Penny and Bobby together."

Just as Tina finished the sketch George appeared at the back door announcing dinner was ready.

They all sat at the table and George dished up, he had made a Quiche with mushrooms, sweet corn and broccoli, there was also melted butter on new potatoes.

"Thought being a farmer you would have a big joint of meat for Sunday dinner, but this looks delicious and tasty." Alice said to George.

"I haven't touched meat since I was a boy, my dad killed my pet rabbit for dinner and I have never forgiven him for that."

"That's awful, how could he have done that to your pet? Tina and I have never eaten meat so we were anxious about today."

"Got loads of eggs from my chickens, I will have to start and sell some of them."

Samuel sat there in dismay, he was not aware that George never ate meat, yet he was a big giant of a man.

"George if you never eat meat why was you sending the sheep to the slaughter house." Samuel asked.

"I wasn't, they sent me a letter suggesting they pick them up and gave a date and I just forgot to tell them I had them for wool and not for killing."

Alice and Tina were regular visitors to the farm and always had their Sunday dinner there, they started to spend more time at the farm than at their cottage.

Mr and Mrs Faye paid Tina to do an oil painting of them, that led to other people asking her to also do paintings of them or their pets.

Alice wrote a book about Penny Bobby and the farm, adding that the author married the farmer. In reality, she just courted him, George would never go down the road of marriage although he had fallen in love with her. Samuel and Tina became very close and Samuel would sit with Penny beside Tina, as they loved to watch her painting her landscape paintings.

One day a letter arrived from Angie asking for a divorce, Collin the man she had gone off with would pay the court costs, as they wanted to marry. The Divorce went ahead and when it was, finalised Samuel asked Tina to marry him, after hugging him then bursting into tears she said yes. George was pleased and suggested that Alice and Tina move into the farmhouse where they could all live there together as a family.

Samuel and Tina were married and it turned out to be a match made in heaven, whereas George and Alice carried on like a couple of lovesick teenagers and were very happy. Sometimes when Bobby got jealous he would push himself between George and Alice, they thought it was funny and cuddled Bobby instead.

They all lived a long and happy life at the farm and the girls helped around the farm but kept up with their hobbies. George made Samuel a partner in the farm and made a good living from the wool and eggs. The girls helped with the running of the farm with the royalties from Alice's book called Penny and Tina's paintings. They also got George to build a big greenhouse so they could sell plants and vegetables.

Love comes from unexpected sources,
when it does grab it with both hands.

THE END

Although, for them it was Just the Beginning.

My mind was full of wonder as I carefully put the book on my bedside cabinet, the past events flashed through my mind as I dropped off into a deep sleep.

The next thing I knew was my mum patting my shoulder, telling me to hurry and get up as I would be late for work. It was strange seeing my dad at the breakfast table and it brought a lump in my throat as I new he would soon be gone again.

All dressed and holding my lunch box I shut the front door and started to walk off to work, I smiled as I remembered the last time I set off for work and spotted the shirt float out of the sky and land on our doorstep. I smiled as I glanced back but my smile soon disappeared as the shirt was floating down towards me. I ran as fast as I could but it seamed to be gaining on me, the bus was just pulling away and I just managed to jump aboard as the doors closed. I felt trapped on the bus, mainly because as soon as the bus reached the next stop the doors would open and the shirt would come in. The shirt was alongside the bus as it sped along just as if it was looking at me, when suddenly a big lorry came past whipping the shirt away. I never saw the shirt again for the rest of the day and I felt a bit paranoid as I spotted white shirts blowing in the breeze on washing lines as the bus sped along on the way home after work.

Great I thought to myself as I sat down to have my tea, the shirt has gone. Feeling relaxed and happy in myself I headed upstairs to bed. I got undressed but when I went to close the curtains I froze because as my hands reached up for the curtains hovering outside my window was the shirt, I quickly closed the curtains and new I could not dodge the shirt forever. It had to be the witch that had possessed the shirt and the terrible carnage she could cause if some one put the shirt on, it was something I didn't even want to think about. I lay awake wondering how I was going to get out the house without confronting the shirt. As the big hand on my clock clicked on to midnight it suddenly struck me, why doesn't the shirt let someone else put it on, why me?

The only explanation I could come up with was I am the original channel for the shirts magic to flow and the only one it can use.

The next morning I decided to phone Clare, to see if Irene or Tom could suggest a way of expelling the witch's spirit from the shirt. Irene told me that the witch's spell backfired on her and it appeared the witch would have to cast another spell to reverse it. The only way she could do that was if I put the shirt on and that wasn't going to happen.

I remembered an incident that happened when I was younger and with a smile on my face, I put a plan into action. Ready for work I opened the front door and spotted the shadow of the shirt moving along the ground from the side of the house.

I quickly shut the front door and rushed to the back of the house, I ran out the back door, down the garden, over the fence and ran as fast as I could to -OLD FRIARS FARM-.

At the blind side of the farmhouse was an outbuilding where two friends of mine lived. Bert and Gladys were looking out of their stable as I spotted the shirt floating across the farmyard towards me. As I entered the stable, I took a squeeze bottle of honey out of my pocket and moved to the back of the stable. As the shirt floated in, I squirted the honey all over it. My two friends's love honey and being goats they eat just about everything. Within minutes the shirt was gone and all there was left was two belching goats. I had remembered the day the farmer had left his long johns on the line and by the time Bert and Gladys had finished all that remained was a pair of shorts.

What a wonderful feeling, I was free at last, even though I missed the adventures Irene had given me. I have a lot of wonderful new friends and Cheryl. Well that is the end of my story about my new shirt.

Strange unexplained things keep happening at the "Old Friars farm" and I keep having to take Bert the goat back as he keeps turning up on our doorstep, but that's another story and I will tell you about that another time in my next book.

-THE REVENGE OF MARION SETTER-

All the very best
Joe Matthews

Printed in the United States
By Bookmasters